EVERY EYE

Persephone Book Nº 18
Published by Persephone Books Ltd 2000

Reprinted 2001 and 2007

First published in 1956 by André Deutsch

© 2000 The Estate of June Braybrooke

Preface © Neville Braybrooke 2000

Endpapers taken from a screen-printed cotton
furnishing fabric designed by Louis le Brocquy for
David Whitehead Ltd's Iberia range in 1956, based on sketches
made in Spain in 1955, reproduced by courtesy of the
Trustees of the Victoria & Albert Museum, London

Typeset in ITC Baskerville by Keystroke,
Jacaranda Lodge, Wolverhampton

Printed and bound by Biddles Ltd,
King's Lynn, Norfolk

ISBN: 978-1-903155-06-6

Persephone Books Ltd
59 Lamb's Conduit Street
London WC1N 3NB
020 7242 9292

www.persephonebooks.co.uk

EVERY EYE

by

ISOBEL ENGLISH

with a new preface by

NEVILLE BRAYBROOKE

PERSEPHONE BOOKS
LONDON

To my mother and father
with love

Every eye must weep alone
Till I Will be overthrown

W.H. Auden 'Another Time'

PREFACE

When my wife died in 1994, there was a confusion about names in the obituary columns. Some called her by her married name of June Braybrooke, others by that of Isobel English – the pseudonym under which she began to publish in 1954 when she was thirty-four. Then, to make confusion even worse, there was her maiden name of Jolliffe and her married name of Orr-Ewing, dating back to 1941 when she married Ronald Orr-Ewing.

Stevie Smith knew her as June Braybrooke, although in 1954 when *The Observer* sent her a batch of novels for review, that included *The Key That Rusts* by Isobel English, she had no idea who the author was. After the review came out, June invited her to lunch – but signed the letter Isobel English. Stevie, in her reply, pretended that she knew who it was. Only when the Braybrookes opened the front-door did she discover the truth.

Present at the meeting, and invited to lunch, was Hugo Manning, whose work I had begun publishing during the war in my little review, *The Wind and the Rain*. When we had no money, he would take us out to meals. Sometimes he would copy out poems for June in his elegant, spindly handwriting:

she put a line from one of them at the top of a note-book, 'Our journey to a far Canaan is always about to begin.'

Sometimes friends do extraordinary things. On June's first publication day, he rang at four o'clock in the morning from Reuters, where he worked on the night shift, to announce that he had seen a not very favourable notice of her novel *The Key That Rusts* in the *Daily Telegraph*. 'Who is it by?' I asked anxiously. 'John Betjeman' came the reply. I had to wait several hours for the newsagents to open up – and by then June had the seeds of a migraine.

Two years later in 1956 Betjeman turned a complete literary somersault, when he reviewed her second novel, *Every Eye*, for the same paper. He declared that the author had 'helped to explode the dying myth that the novel was becoming extinct.' He quoted two sentences to show the power of the writing. First, he chose this to illustrate how much she was on the mark when describing a travel scene:

> Now, we are swinging through France down the lighted tracks where all the night long men in berets and butcher-blue dungarees sweat rough wine and oil through their red and open pores . . .

Secondly, he chose this to reveal her skill in delineating character:

> At least we had the barren fields of our incompatibility between us, which made us better than strangers.

He also informed his readers that though the novel was short, 'none of it can be skipped.'

Almost forty years on, this review was to be recalled as 'a rapturous notice' by the anonymous obituarist of the *Daily Telegraph*. After I had first read it to June, she commented: 'I am over the moon.' Yet within an hour there was a migraine on the way.

June's third and last novel was *Four Voices* in 1960. BBC Television dramatised several scenes and it was arranged that Robert Kee should interview the author. She grew steadily more nervous as this prospect neared, but Kee tried to put her mind at rest by telling her the day before what his first question would be, so that she could write a reply and pin it to her skirt as a prompt. Nonetheless, on the afternoon when she was due to go to the studios, there were signs of an oncoming migraine, for one learns to detect them: one sign is a muddling of words. During lunch, at which she scarcely pecked, she remarked: 'I've got a monkey upside down in my nose.'

When the BBC car drew up outside, she got in with a determined step – and waved: 'I hope they won't ask me to witness the Treaty of Utrecht or anything like that.' Was this a joke? Or was it indication that an attack was gathering? We smiled and hoped for the best.

Most of her life June was subject to these attacks. Yet there were long spells – even months – when none struck. Then, an attack would quickly trigger a row. Booking seats for theatres or operas, or accepting dinner-parties, was always chancy. Her doctor in Hampstead, who saw her in the midst of one, said that it was the worst that he had ever seen. His advice to her was to keep on with the writing, but to avoid the limelight.

Only twice did she ignore this. In 1974, when she won the Katherine Mansfield Prize for her volume of stories *Life After All*, she decided to go to Menton to accept it. Then, in her final years, she gave two public readings of short stories to help the Henry St. John Ecumenical Group on the Isle of Wight. On the rare occasions that newspapers rang, she would say 'I'm a very private person' and hand the receiver to me. In 1974 Kay Dick for several months tried to persuade her to be tape-recorded: eventually June gave in and the tape-recording, in Kay's book *Friends and Friendships*, is the only interview with her ever published. She thought that Kay had a special genius for these things and was an admirer of those tapes which she had recorded of Stevie Smith and Ivy Compton-Burnett. They were included in her book *Ivy and Stevie* in 1971, which she dedicated to us. Kay's tape with June ran for two hours.

Stevie, in her review of *The Key That Rusts* – the first novel, that Betjeman had disliked – summed up June's talent in these words: 'She has a very sagacious and original voice – a voice of our times, ironical and involved, and yet a peculiar voice.' This definition, never bettered, was repeated in both *The Times* and the *Independent* at her death.

The Key That Rusts, when it came out in 1954, went into three impressions. Elizabeth Bowen, who reviewed it, wrote in December to say that she could hardly believe it was a first novel and urged June to submit two short stories, which she had sent her, to the *London Magazine*. John Lehmann turned them both down, as he did all her work. Yet a short story entitled 'Feuille Morte' was accepted by the *New Statesman* by return of post. Later, after her third novel appeared, Elizabeth Bowen wrote once more to encourage her to collect a volume of stories, even if, as had been her own experience, it meant including stories which had not already appeared in magazines.

I read this letter when it arrived, but the first letter I did not see until recently, when I discovered it tucked into one of June's note-books. She had a secretive side to her character, and although we lived in the same house, she often said nothing to me about her literary activities. She did however show me a letter she had from the American publishers Little, Brown about her first novel, in which they asked if a happy ending could be added. She simply said no. More significantly, during these early days of her career, came the news that she had been short-listed for the Somerset Maugham Award, tying for first place with Iris Murdoch's first novel *Under the Net*. In the event the judges were unable to decide who should be the winner, so the prize was given to the runner-up, who was Kingsley Amis, for *Lucky Jim*.

* * *

June, who was born on 9 June 1920, died on 30 May 1994. She was the second daughter of John Mayne Jolliffe, whose father had been an impoverished Welsh schoolmaster who had decided to emigrate with his family of fifteen children from the Rhondda Valley to Australia, to seek his fortune. June, in her thirties, used to dream of writing a libretto for an opera to be called 'To the Antipodes'. Her father had a powerful voice and sang with much *tremulo*. He felt, though, that he could never be a star. His second love was sailing – but, there again, he felt he could never be a crack helmsman. So, he turned to being a businessman and was to grow disappointed and embittered. He could take petty revenges on life, as when he said to his youngest daughter: 'Why don't you make as much money as A.J. Cronin?'

June's mother May Guesdon was born in Tasmania in 1879. The family was of Huguenot stock and proud of it. Her grandfather had come from Brest to Hobart, where he settled and ran a fleet of whalers. May had several brothers and sisters, but when her father was widowed they did not care for his second choice of wife, and under May's wing, when she was in her mid-teens, they moved out to a house on their own. She was strong-willed, striking and had Titian hair. At the age of thirty she read Balzac, in order to teach herself French, which she spoke in a forceful fashion. After her marriage to John Jolliffe at the beginning of the twentieth century, they thought that they and their baby daughter Mitty might live in South Africa: but when they reached Cape Town they decided to sail on to England, where they had a number of relations.

May, before the 1914–18 war, had given an audition to Melba when she was in London; she had advised her to go to Paris and take lessons. May never tired of telling people of her reply: 'I must explain, Madam, I have a young daughter and a husband whom I cannot leave.' When May became my mother-in-law, I soon realised that she had never forgotten the sacrifice of her mezzo-soprano talents which she had felt compelled to make. At the Onslow Court Hotel in South

Kensington, where she lived for some years as a widow, she would re-enact for me scenes from Shakespeare's *Macbeth* – and silence the dining-room. In his great soliloquies – she had little sympathy for Lady Macbeth – she would clutch at the fork before her as if it were a dagger.

June described her upbringing to Kay Dick as that of a 'very delicate' and 'very groggy sort of child.' At the age of two, it was found that she had a tubercular spine and her mother rushed her to a convent in Brittany, where she could have salt-water baths at half the price of those in England. She was confined to a wheelchair – and 'one terrible year' her tonsils were removed under local anaesthetic. The latter left her with a terror of doctors which never quite disappeared. During the nine months of each year which she spent at Saint Jacut-de-la-Mer, her father, riding a motor-bike from Dinard, would arrive for brief stays. In the sports annexe he and his wife would give song-recitals to the boarders, who were mainly lady-boarders.

Then, just as suddenly as June had been rushed over to Brittany, so she was whisked back to London. The French doctors pronounced her cured. The plan was that she should now go to a convent boarding-school at Burnham-on-Sea. But though only eight, she had a feeling that all was not well at home. To Kay Dick she was more explicit: 'My father was getting tied up with somebody.' There was an unsettling background of his women friends drifting in and out – one of whom, she used to recall, lived in a flat off 'Courtfield Gardens, Earls Court'. Early on June developed a keen memory for place-names.

In *Every Eye*, Hatty Latterly, a failed concert pianist, reflects on the melancholy sound of the road called 'Marloes', which links Earls Court with Kensington High Street. In her late teens, when June went down with quinsy in Belgium, she consoled herself by repeating its beguiling French name – *angine de Vincent*. Ten years before, when her mother told her that her new school was in Somerset, she felt that nothing could go wrong at a place which had 'summer' in its name. How mistaken she was! The boarding-school called *La Retraite* at Burnham-on-Sea was far from a paradise.

June was not a Catholic and so was not allowed to go to Holy Communion with the other girls. Yet because she had such a good voice, the nuns pressed more and more solos on her at High Mass on Sundays. Some of the professed nuns, she believed, should not have been let loose among children – in particular one Maths teacher. If the girls in her class misbehaved, they would be forced to stand in a row, open their mouths and have salt placed on their tongues. Then the order would be given: 'Swallow – and offer it up for the persecuted Russians.'

During her last term, when she was sixteen, June asked her parents if she might become a Catholic: 'I did not have any Church of England upbringing. What sort of religious doctrine I had been taught was Catholic dogma.' Her parents refused: her father was not interested in religion, and although her mother never went to any other church than a Catholic one, her loyalty to the Huguenots prevented her from ever taking the step to Rome. June herself did not become a Catholic until a fortnight before our marriage in December 1953.

When she had first gone to *La Retraite*, her father had given her a dispatch case with writing paper, envelopes and stamps. Before she left for Paddington Station, he had promised her: 'We'll make a writer of you yet.' He was thinking of how badly she joined up her letters. His words, though, were to have a prophetic ring – even if perhaps not quite in the way which he intended. For, when she left *La Retraite*, he decided he would send her to St. James's Secretarial College, reminding her that a good secretary is a pearl of great price. Momentarily the impact of this decision missed her, because she could only think of the wonders of the pearl – its iridescence and its pellucid beauty.

Later, when she was grown up, she became a collector of jewellery – and believed that it could be mixed, whether it was inherited, bought at Oxfam or Woolworth's or from Asprey's in Bond Street. When Olivia Manning died in 1980 and left her a legacy, she went out and chose a pair of gold and turquoise ear-rings. As a child, when she had heard the History teacher talk of the Venerable Bede, she thought at first she meant a necklace.

June survived two terms at St. James's Secretarial College. Then she implored her father to let her study Literature. Finally he caved in and Kenneth Allott was chosen to be her tutor.

Allott was a rising poet of the Thirties. In 1937, he had co-authored with Stephen Tait a novel entitled *The Rhubarb Tree*, which became famous because the heroine's voice was only heard on the telephone. To June he dictated notes on James Joyce, whose surname she spelt 'Choice', and on T.S.

Eliot, whose surname she spelt with two l's. In exchange she told him details of the preparations being made for her presentation at Court: 'I said how on the night all the famous photographers kept their studios open, so that debs could turn up before or after they had been to Buckingham Palace. The entrances to their studios were banked high with flowers.' June Jolliffe was presented on 12 May 1937.

Meanwhile, she and Allott continued to explore *The Waste Land*. In her bedroom she would copy out on slips of paper the foreign lines and leave them for her parents to ponder. At night she would go out and see friends who lived in Soho basements, scraped by on the dole and drank out of jam-pots. Eliot's books in their rainbow-coloured covers were regarded as a Bible. June's parents referred to these friends as a *galère*. On other evenings she would go to dances at Sandhurst, or to balls such as the Beaufort Hunt. At the latter she heard a rider say: 'Brute refused the jump. Turned her around. Damned if she didn't do it again.'

These memories were to find their way into the many note-books and diaries, which she began keeping in 1950. In a diary of 1938, which survives, there is an account of how she took a job as a cloakroom attendant at Vasco's Hairdressing Salon in the West End. One day proved enough because there were rats in the basement. The head receptionist of over thirty was 'a hard little blonde . . . with skin like orange peel.' The last phrase was to surface in *Every Eye*, about a French woman who boards the train at Toulouse for Barcelona and whose skin is said to be 'the texture of orange peel'.

My wife usually wrote her books fully dressed – but lying on a bed. *Every Eye* was the exception, for she went down to the dining-room each morning at 11 for two hours: 'I lose a sharp edge after that.' A few lines of the novel were drafted in Ibiza, to which we had gone for a belated honeymoon in 1954. Nor did I read the complete manuscript until it was ready to be professionally typed. Then, after it was returned, she wrapped it in a silk scarf, as was her custom, and delivered it by hand to her publishers – in this case Deutsch. All four of her books were delivered in this manner and the scarves sent back in the stamped addressed envelopes which she had enclosed. She liked to have a decision on a manuscript within a week and rang up if this was not forthcoming.

On the second page of *Every Eye*, Ibiza is referred to as 'the most savage of the Balearic Islands' and, towards the end of the novel, as 'the White Island of Nightingales' – a description used by many of the local people whom we met. How savage the island was, we were made aware of on our first evening when we were sitting in the centre of Santa Eulalia del Rio and saw an American woman stoned by the villagers because she was wearing trousers: she had to take shelter in the bus in which she had travelled and wait for it to return to the capital of the Island.

The novel offers contrasting views of Ibiza: there is that of the picture-book with paths leading off the page to places of serene happiness, and that of blood and sand where blue quilled cocks with sharpened beaks and pared claws fight to the death. Victories are assessed on points – and usually only after each bird is dead. The few tourist agents on the Island in the 1950s kept silent about this.

Hatty, who comes to Ibiza with a husband considerably younger than herself, has been born with a squint, which an elderly lover has paid for her to have removed. She learns: 'one is born with one's infirmities and . . . must carry them always regardless of their visible absence.' This paradox informs her life, with the result that she never sees quite dead on. One is put in mind of E.M. Forster's remark about the Greek poet Cavafy standing at a slight angle to the universe. Hatty, too, sees the world at a slight angle – though, in reality, it may not be her, but the world which is standing at an angle. Inherent in her attitude to 'casting one's bread upon the waters' is her view that although beggars need our material support, they owe us something in return: 'We must reach out to the ends of their poor bound stumps and feel with our bare fingers the true gift of profit and loss.' The sharp-eyed tout of the *Pension Termino* outside the Barcelona station, who picks up Hatty and Stephen, has his own parable to offer on charity, as he drops a *centivo* into the upturned hand of a beggar by the cathedral: '*Mieux que je donne aux pauvres que j'aille à la messe chaque jour.*'

In London, Hattie's lecherous uncle Otway is as much a sinister figure of suspicion as he is a blimpish joke. His new wife Aunt Cynthia, though once a friend to Hatty, becomes more and more a cause of resentment to her as she registers her petty spites. Hatty's own mother is cast in the role of the Greek chorus: 'Don't go to a man's room alone. Don't give them your photograph. They will only make a caricature of it . . .' These are some readings which the novel suggests. Others include a story of oppression by Hatty's elders, or a story of her late gain of freedom by her unexpected marriage to Stephen Latterly.

The working title for the novel had been 'The Path is Overgrown' – the comment made by the student at the end of Act II in Chekhov's *The Cherry Orchard*. In *Every Eye* the journey from London to Ibiza is dovetailed with a journey into the past and the exploration of Hatty's earlier life from her childhood until her mid-thirties. Aunt Cynthia had first told her about the island – and the book opens with Hatty having just learnt of her aunt's death at the Ipswich County Hospital.

There have been many novels based on the premise that life is lived forwards but understood backwards. What distinguished Isobel English's novel from those of most of her contemporaries was a religious dimension. Among her writing friends – with the exception of Stevie Smith and Muriel Spark – few had read the spiritual classics which she had, or had such a familiar knowledge of the Psalms or studied the modern philosopher and mystic Simone Weil, who had died in 1943. In fact all three had begun reviewing her books when they began to appear in the 1950s.

In 1950 I had launched Simone Weil (translated by Mary McCarthy) in *The Wind and the Rain*: in the previous year her work had been turned down by Cyril Connolly for *Horizon* and by some thirty other literary magazines. It was this religious dimension in Isobel English's work which had initially attracted Antonia White and Graham Greene to her.

Yet she had no sympathy for the term 'the Catholic novel', which was much bandied about in the 1950s. Nor was it ever applied to her novels. Religiously speaking she remained a novelist for whom the Last Words of Jesus had a profound resonance and carried an illumination with them. Two lines from the Surrealist artist Ithell Colquhoun, quoted in the novel, also made an indelible impression:

> *Stretch out your hand in the dark*
> *It will be taken.*

These lines answer in Hatty a predisposition to be led and represent a statement of faith.

June often repeated them. She believed that before settling down to work a writer should say: 'Let the Light shine through me.' She was convinced that the veil between this world and the next was a thin one: those on the other side could be 'mobilised' – to use a term of which she and her sister were fond. June had notable psychic powers, but was loath to talk about them, although in her short stories, such as the title one in *Life After All*, she writes freely about psychic matters, and, in *Every Eye*, Aunt Cynthia's son Ted, at her funeral, sees an old friend of the family standing by the graveside whom everyone else knows is too bedridden to venture outside. Ted posts Hatty a 'spooky' letter in which he records these happenings, so as to give her 'the creeps under the hot Mediterranean sun.'

The strands are all pulled together in the final scene, which takes place on a mountain behind Santa Eulalia del Rio. Here Hatty and Stephen go in search of a fourteenth century hermit's place of retreat. At first, it appears a gleaming sugar house. Then, as they draw closer and enter it, they see it is dominated by a single wooden cross, with no figure of a Christus with his arms outstretched to enfold the world. This is the dark night of the soul of which mystics and saints have spoken. On the walls are scratched words with signatures and dates. They are petitions. They are also messages to future pilgrims that nothing in life is ever fortuitous. They hold a special meaning for Hatty and Stephen. Here is one of the most powerful passages in the book:

> Nothing is ever lost that is begun, no word spoken that can ever be broken down to unco-ordinated syllables, no tear shed that will leave only a powdering of white salt. Everything must go on, and on, and on, repeating itself and gathering force for the ever that is still only the bright whiteness of eternity meditated on by mystics and recluses.

* * *

June's first husband Ronald Orr-Ewing, from whom she was divorced in 1953, she regarded as a mentor. It was appropriate, too, that she should dedicate one of her novels to him and their only daughter, Victoria, who was born in 1942. June and Ronald met early during the war, when they found themselves in the same Kensington boarding-house in Campden Hill Gardens. He had intellectual leanings, which, among her family, were regarded as 'awfully bad manners'. Still, her twenty-first birthday was fast approaching, and then she could and *would* marry whom she pleased. Not long after their marriage, Ronald was called up into the Air Force – though he refused a commission. Auden was one of his chosen poets in whose work in the 1940s he tried to interest his father-in-law, but without success. He was much more sympathetically in tune with his mother-in-law, who knew reams of Shakespeare by heart, could recite from Balzac and Browning, and decided at the age of 80 to re-visit Australia, choosing to travel on a cargo-boat.

Ronald was an inspired teacher, although Stevie Smith thought that 'sage' would be a better term. At the Aliens' Office and at Scotland Yard, where he was in charge of the Crime Prevention Committee, he attracted many friends. He was ahead of his time and observed how suddenly the police establishment switched from being in favour of capital punishment to being against it. He also produced a revolutionary White Paper on Prison Reform, and his opening words, on arriving at Parkhurst Jail, have become part of prison-lore: 'I've come to let the buggers out.' His final years were spent as an antique dealer – mainly in Hebden Bridge, Yorkshire, where he was to die in 1988.

He was always seeking talent to promote. Many students he set on their way to high positions in the academic world, and many artists owe their first exhibitions to his patronage. In his early years with June, he told me, she often astonished him with her comments: 'Everything taken out of context can be a deception'; 'I like Rider Haggard, but can't stand Jane Austen'; 'Only our intelligence will save us.' In 1950, when she began to draft short stories, he could not have been more enthusiastic. 'Encouragement is all important when one is beginning to write,' she said. Later, when she said she wanted to start a novel, his admiration knew no bounds. His advice was simple and practical: 'Go out and buy a note-book.' When it was filled, he said: 'Buy another . . .' That was how her novel *The Key That Rusts* came into being. During its progress, he would comment: 'You have passion and style, and compose like a great artist.' In *Every Eye*, Ted, who is partly based on Ronald, offers a variation on these words to Hatty.

June never failed to show Ronald her books in manuscript. Apart from myself, there were only four others whom she treated in this way: Francis King, his sister Elizabeth and her husband John Rosenberg, and Muriel Spark. Muriel chose the titles for June's second and third novels, and in her autobiography *Curriculum Vitae* in 1992, she declared: 'June wrote exquisite novels under the name of Isobel English.'

On June's birthday in 1952, when she was thirty-two, Ronald gave her the *Collected Stories of Katherine Mansfield*, edited by John Middleton Murry. It was in this book that she tried out the pseudonym of Isobel English – 'but in pencil', as she informed the audience at Menton which had gathered to see her receive the Katherine Mansfield Prize. She told them, too, that in her house she had Katherine's sofa, which had been left to her by Anne Estelle Rice, whose portrait of Katherine Mansfield now hangs in the National Gallery of New Zealand. Lying on it, Katherine had said to Anne after a dreadful attack of coughing: 'It's a queer world, darling, but in spite of everything, it's a rare, rare joy to be alive.'

On 1 April 1994 June was diagnosed as having leukaemia. Until three days earlier, she had been working on our life of

Olivia Manning, which was a joint enterprise. Another four days later she was a patient in the Royal Free Hospital in Hampstead – and her condition was serious. Sometimes there would be an improvement, but it was never sustained. In May, in her last month, a group of doctors asked her, on their round of the ward, what she saw from the window. 'A dim light, but there is hope in the clouds' was her reply. In our bedroom at home, among her special books, were Proust, Edward Upward, Katherine Mansfield, Denton Welch, Ivy Litvinov, Forster, David Gascoyne, St. Theresa of Avila and a well-thumbed copy of the fourteenth-century *Cloud of Unknowing* by an unknown mystic. She had him in mind when she wrote the last pages of *Every Eye*. On another favourite shelf she had the works of Ezra Pound and D.H. Lawrence.

Each morning at home when the parcel post arrived, she would shout to me: 'What has the old *Sunday Telegraph* sent you?' One day as I undid their parcel, I shouted up from the hall: 'They've sent *The Letters of Lawrence* – Vol. 4.'

'Can I have a sneak preview?' she asked.

An hour later she called down: 'Come up immediately. I've found something for ever.'

I raced up the stairs.

'Listen', she said as I entered our bedroom: 'Lawrence was travelling and didn't know of Katherine Mansfield's death until about three weeks later. Here is what he wrote to Murry: "The dead don't die. They look on and help."'

That was what we had put on June's memorial card.

Neville Braybrooke
Isle of Wight, 2000

EVERY EYE

I heard today that Cynthia died, last Friday afternoon at the Ipswich County Hospital, just after a cup of tea.

This news has affected me in a way that I did not expect. One minute I was all set with my resentments close-knit and compressed, and the next it was as if a great wave had suddenly crashed shorewards undercutting and breaking into the very foundations of my own life.

So that is what a death is like – to the people who harbour dislikes. The mysterious disappearance involves them as well, and they are left uneasy with a new set of problems to grapple with. . . .

. . . It is six years since I last saw Cynthia, six years since I cut myself free from the inquisitive disapproval; the light unfriendly laugh that always accompanied her sharpest barbs – the honey and the gall mixed to such a smooth consistency that they were inseparable. And yet I should have known the reason for this; I am always talking about a true sense of vocation – the time when I was going to become a pianist – and now once more when I am trying to put together the bits and pieces of my life to start off with a husband who is so many years younger than I.

Cynthia married my uncle nineteen years ago, and from that moment the disciplines of her vocation were applied. I had watched the efforts of day-to-day living drag the tendrils of fly-away hair into an iron-grey cap, the wet forget-me-not blue eyes sink into their bruised hollows to become the colour of stones. The last time I saw her, the most noticeable features were the blunted spades of teeth and the sharp incisors flanking them; these were primitive and vestigial weapons of defence, as if they were the sole means by which she could survive.

'Imagine being able to dedicate one's life to a single person.' Stephen, my husband, is still young enough to be able to speak in this way; 'It's like a talent, it makes up for religion,' he had said. Cynthia was heroic in her selflessness. To eke out the small disability pension of her husband she had gone quietly to work in other people's houses at the rate of two-and-sixpence an hour; and I was not able to support this degree of heroism and what it did to her.

It is strange that this news should arrive today, the eve of our departure. Tomorrow morning Stephen and I are to set off for Ibiza, the most savage of the Balearic Islands. We have been married a year and this is a long-promised holiday. Now it seems something over and above, an involuntary almost predestined mark of respect to a dead person, for it was Cynthia who first told me of this place which must have been when I first met her – about the time of my fourteenth birthday.

It was a Sunday in late August, summer over for me after the return from a bleak two weeks by the sea in the company of rich school friends and their well-meaning parents. These people had regarded nakedness at the sea's edge as a kind of medicinal purge, a self-conscious conceit that was as repulsive for me to observe as to take part in. In damp misery I had huddled beneath the short wrap conscious of my thin arms and flat chest, while the other children bounded about unselfconsciously in the white bathing dresses that they so adequately filled; their legs and arms were the colour of light beechwood in spite of the absence of the sun behind the tight grey sky. I longed for the brilliant camouflage of my cretonne dresses; this material used principally for the making of chair covers lasted for ever, my mother said. One could never sit it out. Sometimes in the past I had questioned the boldness of pattern and design, comparing it unfavourably to the fine sprigged cottons of other children's dresses; now on the hard flint beach at Selsey, I longed for all the wild disorder of enormous moss roses and gladioli. I thought with nostalgia of home and the security of proper covering – the musty smell of the upright piano with its beautiful faded pink silk behind the latticed fretwork.

Once it was over, the sting went quickly away. I could think with detachment of those purple rubbery people and their smell of grown-up and wet wool, leaping about on the windy beach, shouting in wild fulfilment when they stayed the course of a quoit in their pale clenched fists. They became like the wax fairy dolls on the top of other people's Christmas trees who could only draw feelings of envy and inadequacy by their presence; all the rest of the year they were hidden away, covered in black paper. My friends' parents were really quite presentable in their winter overcoats.

Cynthia had walked up the front steps of our ground-floor flat that Sunday afternoon, on the arm of my handsome Uncle Otway. I saw them through the net curtains. I had been practising the piano in the sitting-room and I heard the scrape of their shoes on the stone. I waited for the tap on the glass pane, for he would never bother to summon us with the bell.

When it came I rushed to the top of the back stairs and cried down into the black closed-in hole: 'Mum, it's Uncle Ot and someone I've never seen before.'

My mother opened the kitchen door and let out the light, 'Can't *you* go to the door?' Her hands were covered with flour, 'I don't know why you're so peculiar about the door when he comes. Your poor father's brother. I don't know what you think we would have done without him.'

I turned away, I knew that I would have to answer the door now. Already they were tapping on the wood and flipping at the letter-box.

The strange woman was very small. Coming into the hall in front of my uncle she barely came level with his shoulder. She wore a light gauzy dress tied at the waist by a velvet sash; her eyes were the brightest china blue I had ever seen – apart from Puff our white cat.

'So you are Hatty.' She mouthed the words carefully, like our dressmaker when her mouth was full of pins. Later I was to discover that this deliberate care to sharpen the vowel sounds just prevented the broadness that would have been so much more pleasing to every ear but her own. At the time I thought that she was so small and pretty that I admired even this; it seemed to typify her elegance as did the thin pointed shoes she wore.

My uncle Otway reminded me of a big brown bear in his hairy tweed coat. He flapped his arms around her shoulders; he was her background.

'I met this sweet person last year when I was in Barcelona; she's a native of one of the islands; Ibiza, or do you call it Ibeetha, darling?'

I did not know what they were talking about; once in Barker's tea-shop I had heard a woman singing to the violin, 'Oh! Follow the Big Corona, that comes all the way from Barcelona'. But the island's name simply sank like a stone into my mind.

Cynthia had looked round the L-shaped sitting-room; at the white-painted play-cupboard; at the unmounted tiger-skin that my father had shot in India (you could actually see the bullet holes); then her eyes came to rest on the open piano with its upright stand that held the piece of music which I had just been practising.

'Your uncle Otway tells me that you play the piano very well,' she had said, and at the back of her smile and simple words I could hear the deep billowing voice of Uncle, explaining away my small successes in the Royal Academy exams; my aspiration; my father's death; my mother's struggle for our survival; and how good it would be if I could be 'persuaded, not forced mind you because I believe in people having a will of their own', into going to one of those secretarial colleges that overlooked the saddest part of the Park, where the August sheep in their long matted coats bunched together on the balding grass made one long for the cold winds that would drive everyone back to London and bring about the sameness that united those who had been away with the less fortunate who had never left.

'Yes, I do play,' I answered, 'but I'm only at the beginning.' As I spoke I was drawn like a magnet towards the piano stool.

'Do play something for me.' Her request seemed exactly to synchronise with the fluttering of the thin music sheets as I felt my way through the pile.

'This is an Arabesque of Debussy,' I said as I stood the piece in front of me.

There was a hush – respect and curiosity mingled. She sank into one of the deep armchairs at the other end of the room, beyond the range of my sight. Uncle Otway came towards me, his face creased into smiling lines, just as he had been when we had had our 'little talk': 'I'll turn for you,' he had said as if we were conspirators.

There was nothing I could do but begin. The opening bars were clear and uncluttered; I let the running legato of broken chords follow each other from hand to hand. There was no need to worry even when the right hand set up a counter-rhythm to the left, alone I could play it faultlessly. I had to keep the singing line uppermost in my head, and let the watery greenness envelop me and create the hard pure tone that would shut me away safely from the cloudy grip of interfering relations, the punctuated footfalls from the flat above, and the acid smells of vinegar and cabbage that wafted down the stairs into our rooms about this time every evening.

I was conscious of heavy breathing at my neck; as I neared the last few bars on the page, a thickly furred hand shot out and swept it over. I had not counted on the violence of this intrusion, I struck a wrong note in a chord, and it went through my head like a gun-shot. I did not stop but quickened the tempo in an effort to distract from the mistake. Then I started the slow measured movement that was a rest and respite after the swift flow of the previous passages. The breathing behind me was very close, almost it seemed to disturb and ruffle the short tufts of hair on the nape of my neck; it was nearing the time for the brown paw to strike again. In agitation I turned very slightly, hoping to indicate to Uncle Ot that I could manage on my own. He stood fast, and I saw in that second his eyes crinkle into a concerned smile.

Then I lost my place.

My hands stumbled about incoherently like strangers who had never before touched a keyboard; terrible sounds broke loose, of the kind that tiny children call Chinese music when they strive to express themselves by sheer persistence and force, sometimes by chance bringing together a natural harmony, a beautiful mad sound that can never be repeated. I felt the blood draining away from my face and a still coldness settle round my temples: 'I can't go on,' I cried at last, 'I can't find my place, I don't know what's the matter with me. . . .'

Then my mother came briskly into the room. She looked towards me with annoyance as I sat snivelling on the piano stool; she had obviously been standing outside the sitting-room door and had not liked what she heard. 'That's enough,' she had said. 'Now go and wash your face in cold water.'

When I returned to the room a few minutes later, my uncle Otway was sitting at the piano. His eyes were closed, and he played by ear the same Arabesque. Excessive pedalling blurred the edges, his tempo was extravagantly *rubato* and he struck whole clumps of wrong notes, yet he persevered without perhaps either knowledge or care, swaying from side to side, feeling his way like a blind man through the piece – showing the children how the grown-ups can do it ('and it's not as if I wasn't fond of music myself,' he had said at the time of our 'little talk'). He came to the last chord, then taking his foot off the loud pedal, he rose, and putting both hands to his temples, bowed a Hindustani salaam. Cynthia jumped excitedly from her chair and clapped together her little ringed hands. That was the first breath of resentment.

Yet small lacerations heal quickly when one is only fourteen years old; little more than the shallow warmth of a smile, or the quick concentration of an adult eye, can knit together the tiny hurts of the so recent past. Cynthia turned to me now, with all her little white teeth and dimples alive in her face: 'You're a great reader, Hatty, I can see that.' She looked delightedly at the deep shelves of books, as if she had made a very special discovery; her eyes fell on the encyclopedias and bound copies of *Punch* that my father had left me; she began very cautiously to build me up in my own esteem again. 'I've got quite a collection of books too,' she had said. 'Nothing like these, of course, but I'd like you to come round one day and have a good browse. Some of the books I've kept since I was a kiddy. I still read them. What kind of books do you like best?'

Still cautious but placated almost completely, I answered, a little gruffly I remember: 'I like *good* books,' and then to illustrate the extent of my knowledge: 'I like Rider Haggard very much, but I can't stand Jane Austen.'

6.30 am and Victoria. Stephen's mother, Amy, is already on the platform waiting to see us off; she has brought with her the young girl she hoped that Stephen would marry before he met me. They are dressed almost exactly alike in biscuit-coloured shantung and large coolie hats woven with metal thread. I do not really understand this relationship at all, and imagine that they console each other for the loss they have both sustained through me.

Together, Amy and June have packed all the food for our journey; a whole boned chicken and a sirloin of beef concentrated into the depth and width of a two-pound box of sugar; 'And, there is a bottle of wine too, my children.' Amy is exuberant, her large pale eyes are only just dry; she looks directly into my face as if she is willing me to say something that will unite us all in this great effort to give her son a really good holiday. I feel gloomy and ashen; my conventional thanks are inadequate, I know; but in order to become their accomplices I should have to re-cast my whole relationship with Stephen and see him only as the happy laughing boy whose snapshot on the sands at Le Zoute remains for ever imprisoned behind her eyes.

Stephen flaps in and out of the carriage; his large white hands going like clipped wings. Always at these meetings he is on his guard; watching with a hawk's eye for the outlandish remark that could materialise like ectoplasm from either his mother or his wife. He is a tough ringmaster who keeps us all bucking and prancing right up to the moment of the final whistle blast.

The last few minutes are protracted and uncomfortable. Conversation between people who have not the least idea of each other's whereabouts.

'I love your dress,' I say to June faintly. I mean what I say in that I really do appreciate the texture and cut of the pale silk; but she interprets only the shadows of doubtful resentment in my voice. I am, from her point of view, the *daughter-in-law*. 'Aunt Amy brought the stuff back from China – ages ago. It is sweet, isn't it?'

'Look after yourselves. It won't be long till we all meet again. Be sure to write when you get to Paris.' Amy is willing us away now to speed our return; already she has built a calendar of weeks in her mind and she wishes to apply the first imaginary stroke today.

'Post the letters Mama, don't forget the one for the bank. Look after yourselves.'

At last we are off. Together we lean out of the carriage window. White emblems of peace fluttering from the receding platform as well as from the moving train.

An empty carriage, full of light now; trails of Amy's *Fleurs de Rocaille* still about us. With curiosity we undo the parcels of food. By the time we reach Newhaven, half of it has gone.

It is strange to find the third-class layer of the channel steamer made over in chintz upholstery. The rest-rooms for men and women are separate. Comfortable sofas and bunks line the walls of the women's part; a white-starched stewardess bustles behind the tower of empty enamel basins. There are one or two figures already prostrate on the bunks; eyes closed, jaw clenched, painfully unaware of the smooth sweep of the water, waiting in anguish for the anchor to drop.

Until we reach Rouen, the Normandy countryside seems only an extension of the Sussex meadows. Stunted and wind-bitten cider apple trees have never been affected by the arm of the sea that has reclaimed the land between them.

To begin with, we are a carriageful of nondescript putty-coloured figures. But with the thinning out from station to station, there develop before our accustomed eyes brilliant coloured designs on women's dresses, cyclamen gashes on mouths and headscarves; the cerulean of the sky greased and shining on the eyelids of the girl in front of me.

A young Frenchman and his talkative American mother watch from their corner for a sign of a conversational opening. The man sitting next to me is a Central European; when our passports are examined he pats his own on the cover to draw attention to its British blue and gold. 'Gilbert's the name,' he says smiling, 'Gilbert the Filbert, the Knut with a K.'

I remember this song from when I was three years old; I wonder whose side he imagines we think that he must have been on. There is a kind of lisping audacity about this man, of the sort that one sometimes comes across in visitors to foreign seaside resorts; a thick-skinned *bonhomie* that aspires to knit together all British holidaymakers as 'We Chaps'. His strength is in a way his blindness; he does not concern himself with the clever monkeyish habits of the reserved English. 'Yes,' they will agree to his suggestions, and 'Right you are,' when they are drawn into an impromptu game of cricket on the beach; yet all the time they will be sustaining an implacable unfriendliness whose victory lies in the continued obtuseness of the person against whom it is directed.

Now the fields open up into short-cropped grassy plains; the trees are higher, elegant weeping branches at the broad river's edge. Everything is flat and exposed. No sheltering hollows in which to take cover during a storm.

Why is it that so many topics of conversation are exhausted in a railway carriage? Perhaps it is that to some it is the only audience that they will ever trap in a life. The time is so short in which to complete the final impression, the space so limited, and the rearing up of the cement platform that will end communication, so certain.

Gilbert has begun to explain to us about the business that takes him to Paris *en route* for Vienna: 'There my wife will join me for a holiday, and we will listen to music together.' There is a warm Germanic quality in this explanation that completely wipes away all previous English affectations. The mountains and the garlanded boats on the beautiful river that I have never seen, come suddenly into perspective – this melancholy German romanticism that can never be adequately translated, only transformed into a faded likeness.

The American mother and her son break in on the word 'tide', eulogising over the wonderful cheapness of detergents in England compared with the prices in Paris. Suddenly we are loaded with tips and directions; how not to be done, where to eat cheaply. The young man is so insistent that we feel compelled to follow his instructions or commit treason.

The outer edges of Paris are as frayed and dingy as the suburbs of any great Western capital. We could easily be approaching Euston or King's Cross. This is the first sight of Paris for me, and I look out for similarities to something I already know, some point of contact to set going a chain of background feelings. For Stephen it is different. He can tell the progress of the train with his eyes closed, from his sense of smell alone, it would seem: 'Gasworks, Hatty,' he says sleepily; 'Stinking tunnel,' then, 'Fresh breeze over the waters of a reservoir.' I envy him for his previous knowledge of this city I have never seen. Soon the platform of the Gare St Lazare rolls along the side of us and we are smiling and saying hopeful farewells to the people who perhaps will never cross our path again.

We have booked no room for the night. 'The thing to do,' Stephen has said, 'is to ring up from the station, or else wander about and try our luck.'

I cannot quite bring myself at this stage to the uncertainty of the unknown streets, so we make for a nest of telephone booths. 'It's better,' I say from the advantage of my extra years, 'at least to have some idea of where one is going before we leave the station.'

I am suddenly appalled by the detached guttural tones at the other end of the line that announce, *'Pas de chambres.'* I am about to say something, some kind of word that will soften the precision of those three sharp blows, but there is a crash as the receiver is pushed down on to its distant cradle.

Only in imagination is it rewarding to play on the theme of being stranded in a strange foreign city; then it is delightful, painless, and fraught with thickly jewelled possibilities. Today it is quite different. We are burdened with two pieces of luggage and a carrier bag; the string handle cuts into the skin of my bare wrist, impedes the imagination, weighs me down.

We go down into the Metro. Long draughty tunnels, too near the surface for the controlled silence of air pumps. The carriages rattle in, swinging wildly from side to side of the narrow gauge. There is curly Edwardian scroll-work round the doors; the seats are harsh and austere like the yellow slatted seats of a shooting brake. I sit down on one of the few empty seats, and wonder why there are still people foolish enough to stand. Then I see above the window a large notice that reserves the seat I am occupying for the *mutilés de guerre*. It is impossible now to get to my feet with the train swinging so violently and without the use of my hands.

At St Germain des Près we come out into the summer light. I am preparing in my mind the approach I shall make to the future hotel proprietor. I have known French so well in the past that now with the clouding of years and the lack of use it has become a myth. I think of a thousand phonetic sounds, but no words come to my mind.

Before we go finally into a black entrance that announces Hotel du Rive Gauche over its doorway, I vacillate. 'It's sinister, Stephen – we can't go into the pitch black – it looks like a brothel.'

He trundles me firmly through the door. 'All these hotels are much the same and this looks reasonable enough.'

I feel like letting the bag fall and making for the light again.

Yet once inside, on the black pool of linoleum, there is a soft greyness that seeps down from the upper floors; it is more a degree of darkness than of light, but it makes visible a flight of thick stone stairs and a twisting iron balustrade. There is a bell push on the wall on which is clearly printed the word *Bureau*.

A small room on the first floor. *La seule qui reste.* This hotel proprietor has the keen enough sensibility to know that it is not to her advantage to give me a choice.

Dark red wallpaper sprouting with pearly marguerites disguises the partition that cuts off an extremity of what must once have been the drawing-room of the house: the fine moulding on the ceiling stops dead at the face of one wall. A coarsely carved gilt looking-glass reflects the low-sprung divan with its Eastern wool bedspread. There is running cold water from a tap in the corner, and when we have soaked our feet, we uncork the warm emulsified Bordeaux. Now that we have no weight to bear, we can play a game of possibilities, with the evening ahead. 'Where shall we eat – we might almost move on – find something better. . . .'

Up until now, the word Paris has evoked for me always the end of a mysterious night journey, away from the fishing village in the Morbihan in which I spent most of my childhood; there I imagined the chestnuts must surely be heavier with flowers than any in Bushy Park, the limes in May-time scenting the avenues would scatter their pale winged fruits around the feet of the young men and women hurrying to their glittering white office buildings; there they would carry on a white high-voltaged existence of wage earning that I have never been able to equate to the duller mole-burrowing efforts of office workers who live in the furnished rooms of Earls Court or Bayswater.

Now that it comes to the reality with both feet on the stone pavement of the Boulevard Saint Michel, and later blown by gusts of summery wind through the Luxembourg Gardens, how far are we in reality from the Chelsea Embankment, and do not great cities hold to each other from the core or placenta of all people who live and work in man-made houses?

Stephen takes me to a restaurant on the Seine. It is candle-lit with check cloths, the end of the room built into secluded arbours for those who shun exposure. The main body of the clientèle sit in a double row down the centre of the room: the silent, the tentative, the unrequited in love and those who merely wait in their tired knowledge for the fruit to drop into their laps. Everyone is in some kind of disguise, however flimsy; there are the young who strive to be old and knowing, the middle-aged with their more deadly weapon of self-knowledge and self-sufficiency, and the elderly with all the appearances of infants in their reckless pursuit of immortality.

Stephen and I are shepherded by a harassed waiter to a table in the very middle of the room; we share it with a beautiful-looking couple. The woman's face has the texture of the finest suede dusted with a purple bloom, and her hair is spun silver beneath a crest of white aigrettes. I feel the need to look into my glass; I wish suddenly that I were not so sallow of complexion, nor my hair the dull brown that it is.

'Don't turn round now,' Stephen says suddenly, 'but I think our friend Gilbert is coming into the restaurant.'

To a far table, reserved and respectfully awaited, not hidden from us on account of our central position, Gilbert of the railway carriage walks, and on his heels there follows a girl with all the sweet stooping elegance of her eighteen or nineteen years. As she passes into the secrecy of the arbour-table, I have a close view of the Japanese slanting eyes in the white scented face, the pointed nose with its fine curved nostrils; heavily outlined below it, the sulky mouth is locked now over the little teeth that could bite so deep. Gilbert's eyes look straight at us as he walks, manipulating his big body through the matchwood of tables. We watch him through the forest of wine bottles and stalks of mimosa. He thinks for an instant as he turns, and offers to us the thought of what he will buy for his wife tomorrow. I hear again the sound of sighing violins and paddle steamers on the Danube.

When I was seventeen years old, it was definitely accepted by my family that I had a squint. Up until then I had been cajoled and bullied about my 'lazy eye' – worn corrective glasses and sometimes even a black patch over my good eye. I remember my mother saying to me with conscientious exasperation: 'Now that you *have* this deformity, you must think about it more seriously. You will probably have to have the operation.' That was the ultimate threat. The eye removed from its socket, I had been told, and laid like an oyster on the senseless cheek, while the surgeon with tiny sharp forceps and probes set about tightening the network of muscles that bound it at the back. It was too horrible to contemplate. *It was also very expensive.* I did not find it too difficult to persuade my mother that I might very well overcome it myself with the help of a book of exercises; that people with far more obvious disabilities had tried and succeeded with this system. My face was not my fortune, I assured myself, and from the distance of the concert platform no one would notice my cast.

By the time I was eighteen I had almost forgotten the disability; only when I was confronted with a photograph of myself would I register the shock of this plain face whose right eye turned so fatalistically towards the blind wall of a sharp nose.

My eyes are quite straight now, there is no weakness in the controlling muscles of my right one – yet this has not altered my vision. I am as aware of my corrected squint as if a limb had been removed, leaving only a network of attenuated sensations. I have never been able to give up wearing large brimmed hats; until lately, I did not go out at night without the protection of smoked glasses.

Stephen knows all these things which he regards in his benevolence as picturesque.

'You are extraordinary,' he says to me when I feel in my purse for my spectacle case, explaining that I am distressed and unnerved at the discovery of Gilbert and his lady friend. 'I don't believe you ever see anything dead on, only at a peculiar angle through the corner of your eye.'

He does not know how near the truth he is at that moment, nor realise that one is born with one's infirmities and that one must carry them always regardless of their visible absence.

I don't know what it is that gives to a day the quality of uplift and exaltation. It is perhaps to do with colour or wind or sound that penetrates and stirs the brown depths of the imagination and clears it for receptiveness.

We awoke this morning, and the tone was grey; deep somnolent grey, beginning with the closed shutters on the house opposite that we can almost lean out of our window and touch. That should have given something, that feeling of distance overcome; but the greyness had got into us even before we set foot outside; all the time I was thinking of the obstructive nearness of things. The muscular effort to propel one leg in front of the other was enormous, the street-sounds were grating and one-toned; the same that by yellow sunlight could be lifted to running cadenzas, the accompaniment of winged feet.

We are unlucky over the reservations on the train for Barcelona tonight – and we must take our chance half an hour before the train leaves. Coming out into the prison-yard precincts of the Austerlitz we find it is no place to linger in, have a drink or a cup of coffee; one must hurry away and return at the appointed hour of departure. This place seems only to gain significance for those who are certain to leave it.

Back at St Germain des Près, in the Rue des Saintes Pères, I feel a homing instinct. Walking towards the hotel we recognise several faces that we have seen the night before.

That is the beginning of rehabilitation. We go easily and unspecifically to a restaurant for lunch; it is better and less contrived than the one last night. Already the wariness and stiffness is going out of us, the roll of franc notes depletes itself without our conscious anguish; we are quicker on the fifteen per cent service.

Quite soon the day is over, and we have fashioned it from its grey beginning into something iridescent and unique.

'I'm glad it wasn't easy going when we started off,' I say to Stephen as we drive away from the hotel in a taxi for the Austerlitz once more.

It was exactly five days before my twentieth birthday that Cynthia married my uncle Otway. Everything was very much concealed right up to the last moment.

My mother said to me, after breakfast, that Friday morning, 'You'd better have a new hat,' and before I had time to argue that if she meant it for a birthday present I would rather have a gilt snake necklace, she swept me out of the house in front of her with all the purpose of her strong will driving me up the Earls Court Road towards Kensington High Street.

In the hat department, as she knocked hats on and off my head like ninepins with 'too young, too old', and ruffled my hair into unbecoming puffs over my forehead, she announced suddenly, 'Your uncle is marrying Miller. He wishes us to be present tomorrow morning in Marloes Road at 11.30.'

I wished that my reactions had been clear. At the time I remember only the thick clouding of perplexity as to who this Miller my mother referred to might be, and *why* she should have been so austerely named. The sound of those melancholy words, Miller and Marloes. . . . I have always been a prey to the hidden qualities of colour and scent set going by the impact of sounds. I was enveloped then by the ox-blood brick and the acid and gritty quality of this canal of a road, the workhouse-*cum*-hospital with its dank gardens, and the ancient mulberry trees that shed their black fruit on to the concrete paths like squashed insects, to be dried up by the sun.

'*Cynthia* Miller, of course,' my mother was hissing into my ear. 'Do try and keep your mouth closed, breathe through your nose. It isn't as if you still had adenoids.'

I did not then notice her irritation towards me. I had still been unravelling the mystery Miller, and now she had given me the answer.

'Oh, Mum,' I cried so that the shop assistant moved away discreetly to be out of earshot, 'you sound as if you don't like Cynthia. I think she's sweet. She's going to give me a Victorian bracelet for my birthday.'

'No one has mentioned anything about likes or dislikes,' my mother had snapped back. 'If you choose to be won over by bribes, that is one thing. As for what is suitable, that is quite another. There are some people in this world who do not know the ropes.' And from there my mind, in the grey-felted stillness of this hat department, with the distant sunlight filtering through the netted windows, had been suddenly flooded with vaguely nautical feelings. A certain release, like a ray of ease and lightness came into the whole proceedings, so that my mother and I were no longer even slightly in opposition, but united into an ecstatic front.

We chose a round-brimmed sailor hat with a black band flying away into two tails at the back, which, the assistant explained, could be easily unstitched and a wreath of corn-flowers or poppies make it into quite another hat.

At the Registry Office I had stood slightly behind Cynthia, a token bridesmaid in my green taffeta and bronze sandals. My mother and a friend of Cynthia's were the two witnesses and all through the short ceremony I could hear her breathing through her thinly cut nostrils like an impatient thoroughbred.

Cynthia wore a tight red dress that broke into a mass of pleats just below the hips; her fine silky hair she had gathered into a black chenille snood. She wore no flowers; my uncle had forgotten to order them, she explained outside on the steps; but they were laughing over his forgetfulness as they drove away in the waiting taxi immediately afterwards.

When she appeared in our sitting-room half an hour later, there were three gardenias pinned to her shoulder.

'Rather putting the cart before the horse, Cynthia dear.' My mother had touched her forehead with unmoving lips. I knew that later she would remark on the vulgarity of her pillar-box dress.

'You'll be the next, won't she, Isobel?' Cynthia, since the acquisition of my father's name, had gained stature in her own eyes; I had never before heard her address my mother by her Christian name. Sensible of the narrowing of my mother's eyes, had I not been the subject of this uncom-fortable forecast, I should have tried the prefix 'Aunt' to slip off my tongue. As it was I shut my eyes quickly, then I heard my mother say, 'Hatty will marry when the time comes' – as though by incanting such a commonplace she had added sorcery to good breeding.

My time had nowhere at any given point begun. I had merely left school for the Royal Academy of Music, altered the parting of my hair, and acquired the possession of a latch key. No fresh horizons were open to me beyond the shallow confinement of my own white-painted bedroom and the security of my mother's sitting-room that now housed the only visible change, a grand piano.

'When we get back,' Cynthia continued, 'we'll have some gay old times all together. Ted will bring round some of his friends from the Poly.'

I experienced a certain mounting excitement at the strange prospect of close contact with members of the opposite sex who were not my relations; the dark serge scissor legs, and the almost human expression of the hard blocked toe-caps of their shoes. Ted was Cynthia's son by the deceased Mr Miller. He was very small and did not believe in personal hygiene, or laying down his life for his fellow men. He was six weeks older than I – and our meetings had not been encouraged either by my mother, or for that matter by Ted himself. He was not present at the wedding that day because it was against his principles to condone something so bourgeoise.

'It would be nice,' my mother pushed on, 'if Hatty could get to know a few nice young men from the University.'

Cynthia was not on her wedding day going to allow this to pass. 'My Ted has got a whole gang of pals at King's and the

L.S.E., so we'll be able to make up quite a party, with two undergrads a girl, eh, Hatty?'

There was a white cake that Cynthia had made herself. It had a lumpy roughcast surface like the walls of a new bungalow; the top was thickly planted with silver balls that melted in the mouth from the hard shells of mercury to a soft peppermint centre. I wanted very much to take away and keep in my souvenir drawer the two white doves on coiled wire springs that she had fixed to a sprig of evergreen in the middle of the cake. It was something to do with being young and old at the same time; marriage and independence were within my physical range, but I was nowhere within their orbit.

When they left for their honeymoon, a taxi at the door to take them to the station and from there by train and boat to 'a tiny island, Hatty dear, the third smallest of the Balearics,' I wept without restraint; for the passing of time; for the end of one cycle and the beginning of another. Nothing could ever be the same again.

My mother stood on the front steps prodding me in the shoulder blades. 'I don't know why you're so upset,' she said, 'anyone would think it was a hearse she was driving off in. You needn't worry, they'll be back before the end of the month and then you'll have a whole lifetime to get sick of her in.'

In the pitch-black train at the Austerlitz, we find two window seats; dark strong-smelling leatherette, the floor still damp from the cleaners' rags, and above us the steel slats of the luggage rack.

There must be a great emptying of the mind when one is about to start on a long journey. It is no good clinging to the shreds of last night's anxiety, nor its comforts; everything must be fresh and completely hard at the edges to withstand the future movement and buffeting.

Soon there are four of us committed to each other in the carriage, and when at last the train draws out of the station and the lights go up, shut in and further marooned by the streaming rain on the windows, through a haze of finely curling tobacco smoke, we take stock of each other.

A dark-skinned girl in a pink waterproof jacket has come from Preston; her luggage above us is addressed to Barcelona; she is on her way home after a year's absence. A young French airman who has fitted his back into the opposite corner seat is already trying to get off to sleep; he does not let his hands off the small canvas bag that is his only luggage.

Stephen and I manipulate the quarter-mile of swaying corridor to the restaurant car. Here we order Indian tea; it comes in a little porous but insoluble bag attached to the lid of the metal pot. One can have tea anywhere and always it will give the same feeling of security, but in varying degrees – according to the background against which it is served. Now, we are swinging through France down the lighted tracks where all the night long men in berets and butcher-blue dungarees sweat rough wine and oil through their red and open pores; inside the train, young sleeker-skinned boys drink Coca Cola and smear the pomade of violet grease further into their blue-black hair, whilst they flick with supple wrists and boneless fingers through the pack of cards in front of them. We are like dry stalks of corn in front of all this – and the infusion we drink is as cerebral and exotic as the inhuman Chinese paintings of the Ming Period. That is the outside of it, seen as it were from within. In fact, we are the clumsy and eccentric English who choose to drink a tisane, fit only for invalids. We are here to be fleeced, only slightly less so since the arrival of the Americans.

Back in the carriage they are sleeping; we draw down the spring blinds to shade us from the glitter of station lights and signals that play on the shut-up faces of the other two. Turning and shifting from hip to hip, trying to sink a hollow in the resisting surface of the stuffed seat, now and then we slip away, weighted down by heavy lids. So the hours pass in spasmodic consciousness. When the blackness turns to slate grey, it is Toulouse.

A great shunting and banging of carriage doors. Gingerly we spread our few possessions along the seat in the hope of discouraging other passengers to the carriage, but it is only half-hearted and would not stand up to any robust questioning. I think suddenly of something Cynthia said to me once when we went through the motions of the journey, in her dark back kitchen: 'You always get a baby in at Toulouse.'

It is impossible to slip away into half-sleep when the train is stationary and the corridors alive with people who have been up since four o'clock with all their wits about them.

The airman wakes suddenly, looks out of the window, makes a dive for his grip, then hurls himself out on to the platform.

Stephen has not moved from his twisted position on the seat opposite; his eyes are half closed, but his breathing is slow and regular; his wiry black hair has risen to a point on the top of his head; he looks like a Tartar warrior – someone I have never seen before.

Suddenly there is a black solid mass in the doorway of the carriage, a thick woollen shawl unites a round head to shoulder and arm with no neck visible: '*Y a-t'il de la place messieurs – dames?*'

Stephen contracts from his starfish position, and I gather to my side the few small belongings to make a place. Four people file in, the last, a woman, carries an elderly whiskered dog.

Smoking this first cigarette of the day, bolt upright, head firm on my neck, fully awake, I take a close look at these Mediterranean roundheads. Two are Catalans, and the other two a couple from Perpignan. The French woman nurses in her tight-skirted lap the little terrier called Jooki. She is thickset and her skin has the texture of orange peel; her lips are pale but there is the heavy stain of frequent lipstick applied well above the natural outline of her mouth: there is a suggestion of small-time cabaret about her, of love and violence. One could hear the raucous voice lamenting after having brought down the jagged end of a bottle on the head of a lover: '*Je l'ai tué tant pis pour moi.*'

It is the almost unnoticeable development of the daylight on the strange carriageful and the moving scene beyond the window, that give to the extraordinary sound coming from the mouth of the Frenchman, a frightening almost inhuman quality. He is communicating. I can tell that from the soft words returned to him by his wife; but with each sound that he emits it is as if deep tubes filled up with air and the sound must choke its way up past dust and grit so that finally it is born a tiny and unrecognisable squeak, quite separate and detached from the terrible effort it has cost to produce. He looks vaguely pirate with his flat cheekbones and narrow lidless eyes; around his neck there is a cotton scarf looped into a brass ring.

As the day matures, and the rain of northern and central France dries into dusty streaks on the windows, so we begin to know more of this couple. Their day-to-day reality becomes certified. The man with the coloured scarf is a *mutilé de guerre*. His vocal chords were all blasted away by a shell – quite dumb he was for a long time in the base hospital, his wife tells us. Then they inserted into his neck a bright metal tube to replace the lost vocal chords: this hole, though healed, must remain open; the smuggler's scarf round his neck hides it from curious eyes (anyway he would be unable to support the pressure of a collar). All this she explains to me while he is standing outside in the corridor looking down at the incredible water along whose fringes the train makes its course, so unexpectedly blue to me and yet so much a part of his own tangerine-coloured skin and his thick slower-moving blood.

When the train stops at Carcassonne, he climbs down on to the line; and it is an act of neither boredom nor despair, but of love. Silently he watches the detached engines as they shunt backwards and forwards, the linesmen on their backs, legs curled in like helpless caterpillars as they tap at the stationary wheels with iron mallets. The drab peahen of a wife whose former brilliance she has wished to wash away, even to the silver-leaded line above her shaved eyebrows, sighs as she watches him; it has been a curious technique to acquire, this acceptance of life and death and mutilation, a kind of controlled artistry that goes beyond tears and prolonged feelings of regret. Now she sighs and says, *'Ah c'était son métier avant la guerre, depuis tout ça il travail sur un journal'*. Calmly she accepts that this sedentary occupation is the highest price that he could pay. When he returns to the carriage, they sit closer, there is a visible cleaving together of coarsely worked hands and yellowing skin; the dog-child Jooki springs to her lap to bind them closer, this time she does not bother to arrange the newspaper over her skirt for him to sit on.

It is getting hotter and whiter, and I have given up asking at every sight of the blue, *'Est-ce que c'est la Mediterranée?'*

We take off our coats and let the tiredness dissolve. The train has been cut down to a stubbly finger; it wriggles along the foothills of the Pyrenees, broad and pink-skinned at the base, rising to distant black peaks that disappear into the froth of clouds. I never expected these mountains to be so remote and yet so accessible. We are nearing the Spanish border and the French guard comes round to warn us that we will have to get out of the train at Port Bou.

So, it is Wednesday, and the first for Cynthia below the ground – the cold raw earth lined with evergreens. 'Six feet of semi-detached will do me nicely, dear,' I had heard her say often enough when she was looking for another smaller flat when their lease expired. At last this has been realised as a permanency.

Those who wait upon the act of death and its trappings always say by way of consolation – like the anaesthetist at an operation, 'You will be the last to know about it'. So one must expect that all the elaborate and well-mannered machinery will have gone into action before the awful fact dawns that one can no longer turn over and say something. By now, Cynthia must have accepted her fate; yet attached by the last tenuous earthly ties, perhaps her mind still floats into the warm far-reaching memories of Ibiza, the flowering pink oleanders and the heavy scent of oranges that I have never seen. How are all these things separated in her mind when there is no tomorrow and yesterday? What I do not know now, she will have had to forget by the time I have discovered it.

The girl from Barcelona is slipping back into her real identity, ceasing to be the shy foreigner 'au pair' she carries on a rapid conversation with the two Spaniards, breaking into throaty French when she wishes to make herself generally understood. After the train has pulled out of the mile-long tunnel that marks the border, she makes one last obeisance in our direction, 'We are in Spain,' she says, showing a mouthful of even white teeth.

Quickly we go through the customs and passport office, then round a rustic barrier that is no more than a sheep-pen to a platform where waits the train for Barcelona; it is cinnamon brown, and that is the only visible difference from the French train; but everywhere there is a heavy sweet smell, tuberoses or lilies, yet there are no flower stalls to be seen. It must be seeping out of the pores of the people themselves, men and women alike – even from the numerous members of the Civil

Guard in their nettle-coloured uniforms and tricorn patent leather hats.

I am trying to remember the exact flavour and tone of Uncle Otway's drawing-room in my grandmother's London house, that he and Cynthia lived in before his pension was cut. With this great sheet of plate glass exposing us to the chromium-white heat, and the prospect of three hours to Barcelona, it should be easy to make the heavy Morris curtains draw tight across the window and see again the red watered silk on the walls, the curling baroque frames of the looking-glasses flattening themselves like great golden shells. . . . This was the height of a period of rich fruition when my grandmother had just died, leaving little else but a legacy of beautiful objects, the brief moment before the rot insinuates itself beneath the pink bloom and attracts the pretty blue flies at first one by one, until they are a black cloud settling on the first fur of decay as it worms its way to the surface.

After Cynthia had been married to my uncle for five years, she began in my eyes to assume a proportion; that is to say in relation to the other members of my family. From being a pretty little woman, the kind of mother I would have chosen for myself at the age of fourteen, who later became the recipient of my many hopes and confidences, she had changed to My Aunt, the person most closely connected with the man who had sentenced me to the St Thomas's Secretarial College, and, when that failed, to a high-stool and a metronome that beat against the faulty rhythm of unwilling children whose parents aspired no higher than that they should be able to strum for pleasure at a party.

At this time, Cynthia walked about the area of the cold and unmanageable flat to which they had lately moved, in a loose silk gown edged with dead wisps of marabou; the skirt strained and billowed outwards over her big belly on which she wore a bow, partly as decoration but rather more as a signpost to indicate what was already obvious. In this way it was impossible to ignore the increase of her size. They used to refer to it, my uncle and she, as *the sprog*; and he would pat the bow as the ears of a good retriever, rejoicing at the distention and the great amount of water in which his offspring floated.

For myself, it was difficult to know exactly where to join in. I knew nothing about babies except what I had read in the *St John's Ambulance Manual*, which hardly dealt with pregnancy at all but more with the emergencies of sudden birth. I used to try and pitch my voice to an everyday tone, as if the pat knowledge I could produce for their benefit was a proof of my unsqueamish acceptance of the mystery; but all the time I felt their eyes watched me and pitied me for my incoherence and lovelessness.

I was over twenty-five, and I had come within the core of myself to know that I could never successfully make a real contact with another human being. I knew, without the exercise of much imagination, what happened to women like myself – nothing, except perhaps the increasing weakness of my bad eye that lately seemed to have lost some of its elasticity and power to focus, mainly through neglect to persevere with the exercises, so that it now looked often into the blank wall of my nose almost with relief. Soon the skin of my face would weather and redden as it already showed signs of doing: the pinkness of health, my mother had called it – while I could only think of the small windfalls in the grass that shrivel into rosy immortality because they have never tasted the real sap of life which would have made them rich and rotting at the dip of a branch.

I had just sufficient self-knowledge to assess the extent of my own talent; but I could not accept it as it was. What at sixteen had promised to be the one thing that would protect me and put me far beyond the reaches of human despair had gradually shown itself to be unco-ordinated and intermittent, like a small jewel that has always been hopelessly flawed and can have no intrinsic value except in the eyes of those who seek effect and not perfection. I knew now without a doubt that I would never perform as a serious pianist; that the best engagement I could hope for would be second-rate. All this was evident to me, and yet it was my uncle Otway whom I outwardly blamed for destroying my self-confidence and making me a flop.

To earn my living I taught the piano in a convent school.

One day after tea at home, I said to my mother: 'What do you suppose it would cost to get my eye done?'

As I spoke, I was thinking of the courage it would cost me and the pain (they do not give more than a local anaesthetic for this operation, since complete consciousness is essential). I did not expect her to answer my question at once but to haver a little, perhaps go into the problem of when would be the most convenient time to have it done. When she spoke, it seemed preposterous, as if it was some other being that spoke and not my mother. 'I don't see what you've got to worry about,' she had said, 'you've got on very well as you are; your old eye hasn't stopped you getting good jobs. If it had been a public life, well that would have been different. As it is, with a good brim to your hat, I defy anyone to notice anything wrong with you.'

When she had finished I was sinking into the depths of my despair. Incoherent and seething with malformed resentments, I shouted: 'That's what *I* said, when I was sixteen and afraid. You're using my own words to torture me with.'

Then she had changed again and assumed another character: 'Poor little Hatty,' she cried, 'I wish I'd had the money, if only I'd had the money,' and her weeping was so overwhelming that I was diverted for a little while and set about consoling her for her loss.

I carried this conversation to Cynthia and laid it at her feet: for the moment I forgot the embarrassment of her fat tummy: 'What can she have meant?' As I recalled the scene the motions of horror and indignation mounted; I sat rocking myself backwards and forwards on a kitchen wheelback: 'Can she want me to remain like this, grow old and become a freak?'

Cynthia could not really help me, or so it seemed at the time. She did not attempt to analyse or probe but smoothed it over, spiriting me away through the loopholes she had made for herself into the past, out of the ugly room in which we sat. 'When I was in Ibiza, dear, it must have been – let me see, the summer of 1928 – I never had to lift a finger to do anything for myself; the sweetest little señora used to wash all my undies and keep me as fresh as a daisy, and *all* for love.'

Her dry little laugh as she stood at the deep old-fashioned sink washing the cups, showed up the misty glass of the windows. 'Just a bit of sun,' she sighed, 'is all it takes to show up the drabness and holes in the covers.'

I felt pity take shallow root in me, which was what I suppose she intended by way of a deflection. I noticed suddenly the mushroom coloured patches beneath her eyes and that every time she bent down or reached upwards a little knot of blue veins stood out on her forehead. Below in the street the plane trees were in full leaf. To those who looked up into the green-veined canopy, there was no indication of the thick coating of dust that we could see from the window.

Now, with the easing of my hurt, I thought about the light drifts of underclothes strewn over the floor, of Cynthia slipping her white feet over the mosaic of tiles; the smiling little servant who, like an ancient wool-gatherer, would move from pile to pile restoring order.

And now with the depletion of my uncle's income, a retired lieutenant-colonel's disability pension, all these past scenes were hardening into the immobile permanency of picture postcards – stills, like lantern slides, that required only a trick of light to bring them to life. There was little sign of ease or leisure in Cynthia's life at that time; only occasionally could it be detected in the supple flexing of the wrist as she held, poised for an instant, my grandmother's boat-shaped silver teapot over an empty cup.

The heat increases. We are inside a furnace with the damper out. I am immensely thirsty and Stephen smilingly offers me the last drop of the wine that we have carried so far; it has undergone another change and now tastes acid and astringent, like a vile tonic. It makes me want to spit, but I find that I have practically no saliva.

Thinking about the approaching city – white, as I imagine it will be, but not in any way smooth and lit from within, but rather more opaque and chalky, with dust rising in the streets in thick hot clouds at the stirring of a wheel – all this produces in me a certain inertia and predisposition to be led:

Stretch out your hand in the dark
It will be taken.

At twenty-five then, that must have been the moment, the peak of the affinity when it seemed that Cynthia had it in her hands to bring out the sun from behind a cloud and focus it on me at will.

It was late summer, on the fringes of autumn, with the leaves still fast upon the trees; yet here and there a cobweb skeleton leaf in the grass showed where the prematurely aged had escaped even the process of decay; there was no sign as yet of the damp brown drifts, only the perfection of this in-between season.

Cynthia was within two weeks of expecting her child. I had bought myself a floppy leghorn hat to wear at the party.

'We must have one last fling before I go in,' she had said, and we had worked through the list of names as she calculated the quantities of food and drink that she would have to order.

'Teddy is always such a help with the difficult ones,' she had said, not so much as a reiteration of ancient maternal pride, but one of almost filial dependency that must have been fostered by the very instability and precariousness of her financial position with my uncle.

'I wish you two could make a hit together, at least you could go to concerts; it isn't as if he had anyone else in tow.' Her efforts to produce a family unity had been boundless. Ted and I had met frequently in a neutral background: a flat that was as much his mother's as my uncle's. It did not bring us any closer.

He had never heard me play the piano, and I had nothing with which to disprove my inadequacy. 'Hatty has the L.R.A.M.,' he used to inform people.

'She's *so* musical.' But this announcement was nearly always in relation to having just been to 'an out-of-this-world and magical performance' by someone like Cortot or Pachmann.

Slowly, however, I began to accustom myself to the fruity tenor of his voice; the damped-down yellow duck's-tails that seemed always the same length; the area of his emotional experience that spanned the great unknown jungles from Torrington Square where he lived, to the World's End, Chelsea.

We had, at the suggestion of his mother, made one or two Sunday excursions into the green belts of outer London.

A terrible day, I remember, at Boreham Wood, over-shadowed all the way by the living presence of George Orwell. We had arrived at the village after a long and silent walk through the Hertfordshire lanes. Ted had hardly opened his mouth, and this unnatural behaviour on his part set me to cast about wildly like a mad woman for something to say. I already anticipated the kindly inquiry from Cynthia when we got back: 'Well, what did you see, what did you talk about?' I *had* to find the one thing that would show deep thought and observation, an apologia for the humiliating void in my mind. In the difficult gymnastic of getting across a high stile – it did not enter his head to help me – I stopped, and called out to where he stood in the middle of the field, 'The swallows are flying low, that means rain, doesn't it?'

He did not answer my question, he did not even turn and laugh at the peculiar ineptness of the remark. He merely walked on towards the main road, and I thought: perhaps he is afraid for me because of my nervousness and twenty-five shrivelled years. Or perhaps he never heard.

We had arrived at Boreham Wood at the moment when the street lamps were turning everything a harsh yellow, their broad shafts cutting into the sooty evening.

In the teashop there were two other couples besides ourselves, and it was here that Ted began suddenly to orate and soliloquise. 'You can see that shrimp of a girl over there in the fawn belted coat, Hatty?' and when I turned in the wrong direction, 'No, not that one, over there with the brown-haired chap. Well, I will tell you what he is thinking as he watches her rubbing together her chapped hands, self-consciously spinning into view the tiny sparklet on her left hand that she has lately acquired – a ray of hope. . . . He is peeling away the years ahead until he sees her an upholstered, better-moulded

Hilda (that's more than probably her name), not the uneven bit of girl who always suffers from extreme of heat or cold, but a subdued impervious woman with neatly coiled hair, in a well-fitted jumper suit sitting behind the electroplated teapot and doing the honours without a grizzle or a smile. . . . My God! it makes me sick all this cannibalistic gentility! Bourgeois clutter – and what is it bloody all for, I ask you?'

After this spate he collapsed, fell inwards into his own thoughts, devoured two doughnuts, and left me mercifully on my own, isolated and unnoticed.

So there was Ted then, at the top of the list amongst the family beside my own name; at least we had the barren fields of our incompatability between us, which made us better than strangers.

I arrived late at the party – the prerogative of the very worldly, or the uncertain, and steered my way on new high-heels towards Cynthia, who sat in a Victorian nursing chair. She bloomed out of it like a blue hydrangea. There was a tall man standing beside her, and he had to bend himself almost double in order to reach her ear.

After I had kissed her she took my hand and, giving a slight tug to this strange man's coat to draw his attention, said, 'This is an old friend of the family Hatty. Jasper Lomax; my niece Hatty Skelton, Isobel's child.'

He straightened himself and smiled vaguely at me; then I noticed that he was quite old. Apart from the thick hair that might have been prematurely grey, there were deep trenches in the flesh that ran from nose to mouth; his cheeks had fallen away like canvas tents that had lost their supports. 'Jasper has known us all for a very long time. You knew Jim too didn't you?'

At the mention of my dead father's name I looked at this strange man more closely and with greater interest. She did not give him time to reply then, but with, 'I'll leave you two together, there must be so much for you to talk about,' she sailed across the room like a small galleon floating through her guests.

'Let me see,' Jasper Lomax was saying, 'I knew your father in India yes, but I think we've met before too, if I remember rightly.'

He had a thin squeaky laugh that seemed to have no connection with the broad high shoulders and big sunburnt face: 'I called on your mother once, it must have been on a leave during the fourteen-eighteen war; she was living in a pretty little house near Victoria Square. *We* were introduced and I was allowed to crawl with you in your pen; you were a tough little blighter and tried to kick me out with the points of your leather boots.'

'Shoes,' I said instinctively correcting, then regretted it.

Yet he seemed not to mind and went on talking in the same tone. 'Oh, well in my youth it was boots for boys and girls alike, so I expect it always will be, in my mind.' He had not spoken in the least sharply nor seemed put out by my too quick interruption, and I was grateful for the steady continuance of his reminiscence. In a way it forged the first frail link, kindled a hidden warmth with someone I had never seen before, but who was remotely connected with my family and childhood. That was the beginning.

I remember so clearly the beautiful translucence of his saxe-blue eyes, the healthy brown pouches that ripened into the fine veined cheeks. I looked out, it seemed for the first time, with the control and focus of both my eyes.

'Look here,' Jasper said to me after we had been separated and met again later in the evening – during which time I had never let the sight of his big grey head escape me, 'won't you take pity on an old buffer and have a bite of dinner with me one night?'

I could afford at that moment, and I suppose that therein lay my strength, to register surprise, minute disgust at the ugly picture that those words created in my mind. 'I'm in the middle of my Royal Academy exams,' I said. 'I teach music at a school, I expect Cynthia's told you' (I imagined both in arrogance and humility that he would know all about me from my uncle and his wife). 'But I'd like to though when the rush is over.' I watched the flicker of interest in his eyes; I had guilelessly held back in this game of manners, not jumped like a pup at the sight of a sugar lump.

He said, 'Well that will be simply splendid, I shall look forward to it. Will you take it that I shall contact you through your aunt and uncle?' He gave a strangely old-fashioned bow that was as becoming to his height and age as it was self-conscious in its precision.

It was not what I had expected – this cheerful acquiescence; nevertheless I went away from the meeting relieved and a little satisfied with myself. Really it was cheek of the old boy – he must be at least fifty if he was both Father's and

Uncle Ot's contemporary; yet this very fact I supposed was reason enough for him to ask me out.

A few days later I discovered that he was a distinguished traveller. I saw his name in the paper as guest of honour at a dinner given by the Royal Society of Archaeology. Seeing the words *Jasper Lomax*, separated from the reality of his body, was the magical turning-point; age fell away from him, leaving only the bare bones of manliness; the high-arched eagle nose and the imprisoned bravery within the skull.

It was nearly two weeks after the party that I had the sudden and impulsive desire to telephone him at his club. He was not there, they told me; he called in only occasionally for letters and messages. I put down the receiver quickly before they had time to ask me my name. Like many people who are unaccustomed to constant use of the telephone, I endowed it with an extra sense; *I was certain that the black mouth could see*. Sick with shame at the boldness of my action, I imagined that the call could be traced; I could have bitten my tongue out and beaten myself. Now at each subsequent ring, I waited for the frightful snub that would be delivered to me through my unknowing mother, for I was determined to never touch the instrument again.

Jasper telephoned the following Sunday just before luncheon. 'I've been thinking,' he said, 'that your prison sentence must be nearly up; what about next Wednesday? I've been lent a car for the rest of the month, we could go for a spin down to Maidenhead, have a bit of dinner at Skindles, and look at the river. September's a fine month for the river. What do you say?' He did not mention anything about my abortive call to his club. Perhaps he had not been told.

To never have the exact knowledge of one's position is the predicament of human frailty. Compassless, to see the beckoning lights, one advances to find that there is nothing there but a reflection in the deep-rooted blackness. I remember the third of my closely spaced meetings with Jasper.

We were travelling down the spine of Campden Hill, just at the bottom, taking the right bend from Phillimore Gardens into Argyll Road, the taxi lurched bringing into sudden close contact the fine granulated texture of tweed with my bare arm; his front teeth grazed the middle of my upper lip, my neck arched stiffly backwards against the granite plumpness of the black upholstery. I felt like a rabbit hypnotised in the full glare of the headlamps. Instinctively I drew up my knees, rigid as the ancient burial position of the Incas; I could not move even after the taxi had straightened on its course and Jasper, insidious as an outgoing tide, had withdrawn into his own corner.

Out on the pavement it was bright and blue, the same as yesterday and the day before. Jasper pushed his large-brimmed hat to the back of his head with a reckless corner-boy gaiety, and said, 'Well, my sweet, when shall I see you?' As he spoke, I could hear my mother's voice pounding in the back of my mind: Men, men, men. Men in their cups. *In vino caritas*. Don't you believe it. Don't make yourself cheap. Don't go to a man's rooms alone. Don't give your photograph. They will only make a caricature of it. Draw in a moustache. Hold it up to ridicule in their messes – or wardrooms.

'Why are you looking so perplexed?' Jasper's voice came to me now through the spiderwebs of fears and doubts; he took my hand. 'I can't stop now, but ring me early tomorrow. Promise?'

He was drawing away, eyes already calculating the distance from one side of the road to the other, waiting for the two cars and a bicycle to pass on before crossing.

'Jasper,' I called out suddenly, 'tell me why you want to see me again?'

He had nearly reached the other side of the road. When he had mounted the other pavement, he turned to face me, the road was now quite empty of people and traffic, yet he cupped his hands to his mouth to amplify his voice: 'Let's say, because I LOVE YOU.'

The words carried right into the soft part of my brain and stuck there like three neutral stones. I suppose that I must have stood there with my mouth open, my bad eye focusing all over the place in an effort to materialise him again in the gap which he had left. This was the first time that anyone had ever said these words to me; the first time, and they were no more active than fizzy lemonade. I wanted to reach out and extricate them from the smutty stucco frontages of the ugly houses, save them from the smell of petrol and the dust-thick sun of two o'clock of that September afternoon

2.15 pm and Barcelona. The journey has been a slow and glaring exposure; our carriage filling up at every step with brown glistening people; curious smiling faces, the widespread skirts settling like sheathed umbrellas; then the fluttering of their pleated paper fans to stir up the atmosphere and give a feeling of movement.

In my lilac angora jumper, my face suffused to a sugar pink, I am like a decorated fondant that will quite soon begin to melt into the deeper more treacly textures of the skins around me.

The Catalan girl has at last relinquished her rainproof jacket; the tops of her arms, in spite of Preston, are still tobacco brown in colour; she speaks not a word of English now. Only once she leans forward to offer me a Capstan from the store she has bought on the channel steamer.

If I have ever supposed that Barcelona would hold within its city walls anything approaching the elements of cosiness, either cobbled street or withdrawn courtyard, where one could sit in comfortable security and absorb to one's capacity, I am grievously mistaken.

We are hurled out of the high-stepped train on to the platform, alive as a beach shelved with a fish catch. I realise that after we have said goodbye to the girl from Preston there will not even be the possibility of making vocal contact with anyone. Stephen is ahead of me. 'Where can you suggest we get dinner?' he asks as we use the rounded edges of our baggage to push our way to the barrier.

She smiles back at him blankly – a little doll with the taut strings of her box barely snipped: 'I'm afraid we don't eat out in restaurants in our family, but I will ask someone in a minute.'

I turn away under this echoing arched dome of glass, this white-hot glittering palace, and mentally detach myself from Stephen and the girl who are carrying on a rapid conversation in French. The idea of the empty hours of the siesta which will be at our disposal, the liberty to go to any far hidden corner of this great commercial city, is like commitment to a rudderless boat without anchor.

There is a commotion of voices quite near me; a quick fire of question and answer. Stephen and the girl have been joined by a ferret-faced boy across whose peaked cap is written, *Pension Termino*. He is smiling and shrugging his shoulders, indifferent, yet insistent: the perfect patience of an angler, as we are later to discover. He speaks a harsh inaccurate French and some broken English, but it is an element of contact between us. I do not like the scaly quality of his reddish eyes, they remind me of a lizard's whose low temperature can never be increased even on the most sun-baked wall. The girl is shaking our hands and saying finally, 'He will take you to a place where you can get dinner for twenty-five pesetas each.'

I want suddenly to hold on to her and say, 'Thank you, but no, no, no.' But I am too late, and she is swallowed up in the crowd.

The boy has now both our zip bags and is leading us out of the station. I start to speak to him in French, cutting through the dust and phlegm that has collected at the back of my throat, forcing up the words, to discover where he is taking us. It is quite simple, he says; he understands perfectly what I say, and is taking us straight to the hotel of his *patron*.

'Stephen, the shipping office, you won't let him forget the shipping office?' I insist, some of the urgency already draining out of me; he answers that everything will be all right and that there is plenty of time. He too appears rapt away, hypnotised by the penetrating glare; so we move inevitably

46

down the half-empty tramlined streets. We follow this strange youth almost in a trance, yet all the time I know in the back of my mind that there is something I will have to insist on – later.

How to get over the hump of the afternoon? It is too hot to walk and I wish now that I had not worn high-heeled shoes. The thing to do after this little journey will be to find somewhere cool where we can sit and drink.

We penetrate a dark entrance through an archway on the far side of a big tired square. There is an inner courtyard and, hanging from the walls like giant creepers, a complex of iron stairways. On the third floor up, we find a glass door and painted across it *Pension Termino*.

Inside the little lobby of the *pension*, we cause a great deal of excitement; the boy who is the trusted fisherman on the platform for the incoming train from France hands us over. I notice that the bright black eyes of the patron and a full-breasted serving girl flit from our canvas luggage to our new portable typewriter. They indicate an empty table, and the girl starts rapidly to alter the position of the cloth, so that the stains will be less noticeable, and to lay out the knives and forks.

Stephen insists in French that we have already eaten on the train; that we will drink some cold lemonade. There are Victorian glass cruets on the table filled to the brim with oil and red wine-vinegar. Everyone around us is eating fried eggs; they scoop out the yolk and fill it with pools of olive oil: it is not to be wondered that their skins should be so glistening: their hair as flat and shining as the silk top hats of city businessmen.

The lemonade is colourless and cold, thick spoonfuls of sugar like fingers of frost stick to the inside of the tall glass; it is the most cooling drink that I have ever had. We leave the little hotel on the understanding that we will return for dinner at six: the boy, who is called Ramon, has taken off his uniform hat; we are no longer of interest to him as he looks concentratedly towards the kitchen, awaiting his three o'clock meal that is part of the payment for his labours on the station.

We shall sit in the open until four o'clock when the shipping office opens. There is a café on the pavement – a few iron chairs scattered round a bar counter. Under these shadowy arches of the square below, there are all levels of beauty and nightmare. We sit drinking more of the colourless sweet lemonade and watching.

Down one sharpened vista, we can see the staffs from the big commercial houses round the docks taking their lunch in shadowed respectability. In the near vicinity, almost at our feet, there is the scattered and squalid refuse from a one-windowed shop that sells only fish. Outside here, the people are like the mutilated debris hidden away in the arches: fishes' heads, with their mouths still open in a last effort at survival, and the wooden-legged no-eared riff-raff who work as they can on the cargo boats. There are people always in life who accept the very act of drawing breath as a gift of God, and each sense or limb that is denied them only serves to accentuate this gift. Finally, they become as disembodied angels, geniuses or idiots – almost incapable of communicating to the outside world. We should give to their material support, but they owe us something too: we must reach out to the ends of their poor bound stumps and feel with our bare fingers the true gift of profit and loss.

The boy Ramon comes out into the street and recognises us. Without invitation he sits down at our table and orders for himself black coffee and cognac; there is something permanent in this attachment and Stephen says that we must soon go and book our places on the boat for Ibiza. '*A bientôt,*' we call out; but to Ramon this is no farewell.

Now we walk without knowledge of our direction, slightly behind Ramon until he turns round and points up to a tall spire; through the narrow gothic streets we follow him to a sandy space when suddenly we are at the bottom of the shallow flight of steps leading to the great entrance of the cathedral. Wedged in between other buildings the mass of creepers give to the ancient stonework a feeling of preserved ruin.

Inside, it is like sudden blindness after the glare; not a beam of light until the eye accustoms itself and discovers the rows of spluttering candles in front of the shrines, and the red swinging lamp at a side altar.

I do not yet understand the arrested Latin philosophy that is Spain. I do not understand the essence of their being: the blood-letting and the blood-staying that is part of the bread of their existence. It is perhaps a deeper faith and acceptance, that goes beyond the elaborate traceries of our northern minds. All the time in Spain it is the pitting of strength against strength; and this technique is developed to such a point of perfection that the loser must not witness his defeat. Bulls, royal-blooded, stampeding and prancing, wait ultimately only for the jewelled dagger between the eyes.

Blue-quilled cocks with sharpened beaks and pared claws spread their wholeness over the small sandy pitch, and nearly always expire side by side, their victory assessed only by points – after they are dead.

As we come out into the light again, the boy Ramon drops a *centivo* into the upturned palm of a beggar: '*Mieux que je donne aux pauvres,*' he mutters, '*que j'aille à la messe chaque jour.*' With this parable on charity, niggling doubts of his innocence begin to disperse.

'Gaudi,' I say suddenly spirited, 'how far to the Sacrada Familia?' For this strangely hideous temple sprouting stone cacti on its spires of which I have seen so many pictures, cannot be far to reach. Ramon does not answer my question, his eyes empty of interest. 'Gaudi,' he says, 'very old man, he stood where a tram.'

Stephen is on another track; with smiles and hand movements he is asking: 'And do they have dancing before the high altar on feast days, *pour les fêtes de l'église?*'

Pin-points of interest return to the boy's eyes; the words have struck some chord, let loose a deep longing in the thin hard mind of Ramon. '*Fêtes,*' he says like a word of exultation, '*Feria.*'

Suddenly we are in a taxi, sailing away from the crazy toppling streets into wider spaces; tree-lined roads rise out of the nest of ancient stone, a feeling of being above sea-level replaces the city claustrophobia. The taxi slows down at a turnstile and there is a roar of loudspeakers as the shock of amplified music booms in our ears. We are at the entrance of a huge industrial fair.

'*Il feria!*' shouts the boy joggling his head to the music; and Stephen digs into his pocket to find the nine pesetas for our three entrance tickets.

Inside, it is how I have always imagined Olympia; a place I have avoided going to all my life in London, but am incapable of missing the first day in Barcelona.

A whole hour of deafening stupefaction; now and then a glass of warm beer at Ramon's request, then we are in a grey upholstered taxi swinging back to the *Pension Termino* for our early dinner.

One last drink in the square before we go up to eat: the opaque clouds of absinthe are stained coral red by the addition of grenadine, before the water.

At the quayside there are two white boats rocking like birds on the sheet of water. Ramon pushes us towards the nearest, and we walk quickly, for it is nearly seven, the time scheduled for it to sail. He goes before us to speak to a woman clerk who sits in a closed-in kiosk; then turning round he beams a reprieve: '*Le bateau ne part qu'à onze heures,*' he sings, swinging his narrow hips – clipping two coins together for the sound of castanets; '*ce soir vous verrez le jolie cabaret, vous aimez le flamenco, Madame?*'

Suddenly I know that this is the moment of insistence that I have been waiting for all day; simultaneously I see the word *Palma* painted in black on this waiting boat. Running forward I shout to the woman, '*Ibiza, le bateau pour Ibiza.*'

She becomes galvanised into action and jumps to her feet; then she points excitedly to the other boat whose funnels are belching clouds of smoke.

We run like the wind and the boy with us. The decks of the boat are black with passengers and the gangway is beginning to soar upwards: the crew throw across a plank when they see our hurried approach and we hurl our luggage all but the typewriter on to the centre deck, then with care and amidst loud cheers from the other passengers, we walk the plank.

The vanquished Ramon shrugs his shoulders and withdraws; he has after all only lost what he so nearly won, on points, seconds on the clock. Stephen leans forward over the rails and holds out a crumpled fifty peseta note. He takes it quickly without a word, then disappears into the crowd not to tempt providence further.

How can one ever know the extent of one's own or another's victory in the hidden battles of the heart? Words and gestures extracted from their context become inflated to gigantic significance, then later as precise and moribund as a flower specimen pressed into the leaves of a book when the life-giving stamens are blurred to a small yellow stain over the print.

I had thought at the beginning of my love for Jasper that it would sustain a quality of agelessness and endurance; that it would become finally as sweetly preserved as a bowl of dried petals, from which I would be able to draw strength until I died.

Cynthia, who was more knowledgeable of the past, knew differently. She was also forward-looking.

I played a game like this: 'Of course, there's nothing in it as far as I'm concerned,' when she chided me about my beau.

'I only hope he doesn't take it too seriously, it's so nice to have him for a friend.'

Whether she accepted these insincerities or not, I never knew; plump as a pouter pigeon, in spite of the removal of a ten-pound son to the cradle in the corner of the room, she was well enough padded against emotional draught to be able to reply, 'Well, I think he's very taken with you dear, but you know what *men are*.'

I, in fact, knew nothing; not even remotely to what she alluded. I thought in my wisdom and hopeful innocence that there must be some hidden answer to what people were really like contained in a simple word. It was like searching for a magical incantation, for the essence and elixir of life, believing that it still existed. At ten years old, my uncle Ot had answered me when I begged a cigarette for myself, 'Go into the garden and find for me a flower that has all the colours of the rainbow in its petals and that smells of Christmas turkey at its heart, and I will give you a cigarette in exchange.'

Now, Uncle Otway reflected what should have been my mother's prerogative – had she been more fully aware of my new relationship. Having in a sense produced the rabbit out of the hat, he now sought to force it back. He was thunderously disapproving of my meetings with Jasper, whom he would no longer invite to his flat. When he saw me alone it seemed that metaphorically he was trying to force me back into a cradle that I had never been particularly anxious to leave.

'You're a bloody little fool to play around with old Jasper. I happen to know more about him than you do. You seem to forget that both your father and I were with him in Quetta before you were born.'

I was outraged by the violence of his attack, thrown suddenly into a seething whirlpool of doubts and resentments.

Ted was about to witness these scenes, sometimes hovering in the background with Cynthia whilst the arguments took place. Now and then he would mildly tease me about Jasper, but I think his feelings were well disposed and for my own part I felt easier and more communicative in his presence than I had ever done before.

One day before tea, my uncle produced from a shelf a book containing something he said that would interest me very much. Uncertain of his humour, for there had always been a horrific element in his jokes, I waited tensely.

'It's a poem,' he said at last as if by prolonging the uncertainty he would have us more fully at his mercy when the time came – 'it's a poem and the poet, if you have retained your education, should not be unknown to you; as to the subject, let it apply to whom it may.' Then he cleared his throat and boomed:

Some men to business, some to pleasure take
But every woman is at heart a rake.

There was no doubt in my mind at the time but that the attack was against me. Cynthia and Ted sniggered into their tea-cups, while Uncle Ot, having made his point, rubbed his hands jovially together and cut deeply into the slab of fruit cake.

I was, I remember, paralysed with misery and self-consciousness, desperately intent on controlling the tears that were already beginning to slip down my nose, without the use of a handkerchief, I stared into the hard brilliance of the central light bulb until it cured and dazzled me. But that was the end of it, I thought, as far as I was concerned: I would never be able to ask Cynthia for her advice again, now she had definitely established herself as my uncle's pawn.

The last thing she had said to me as I got my coat on was: 'Well, you really do ask for it Hatty, with that soulful look and mop of Rossettian hair; your uncle doesn't mean any harm; he takes the stuffing out of all of us. Have a heart now.'

Ted came out into the street with me and we walked some of the way home. 'What a terrible pair,' I said, 'quite heartless, like a couple of stone images.' I forgot about Cynthia being his mother, and went on fanatically: 'Do you think it's insane jealousy that makes Uncle Ot go on as he does? A kind of incestuous affection; he tries to kiss me at the front door in a – I don't know how to describe it – lingering way. Last week he hung over the lid of the piano when I was playing a Liszt variation.'

Ted stood back on his worn-down heels and laughed at me with real pleasure and surprise. 'You're coming out Hatty, really you are. I always imagined that nothing much went on in your noodle except a ditty-bag of old maidish fancies and a sentimental attachment to the better known arias.'

Strangely, I did not mind it when he said this, I was buoyed up, insulated against everything by my present obsession.

'What do fathers and uncles want of their offspring, Ted?
Does Uncle expect me to go on like a perpetual schoolgirl,
bringing my prep home after tea for all eternity?'

But he did not answer my question, nor did he try. 'It's
perfect Cocteau,' was all he said as he climbed on to his bus
and was carried away towards the Euston Road.

Cynthia tried several times in the near future to smooth
over the upheaval. She did not refer directly to the scene, but
tried in her usual way to divert my feelings of resentment
towards her and Uncle, by returning to a neutral territory that
was both a pleasure for her to recall as it was for me to hear
about it. I think that she regarded this island of Ibiza as a kind
of emotional sanctuary. 'You mustn't worry too much about
the present Hatty; the only consolation I can give you from
my great age is that everything diminishes with time, unless
you want to keep it alive. When I had my job teaching in
Barcelona at the language school, I was a bit like you. I had a
marvellous time. Mind you, I had to scrape a bit to send back
the money to Mother, who was looking after Ted.' She drifted
away forgetting, it seemed, the purpose of her reminiscence.
'I was in the early thirties and I never expected anything
to happen that would change my way of life. I thought I would
go on teaching English in Spain and coming home once a
year until I'd saved up enough to settle down in a place of my
own; in Ibiza, I hoped.'

I remember her now as she had been when I first saw her.
The picture that had been taken with the unclouded lenses of
a fourteen-year-old's eyes had gained in the intervening years
another dimension; I could see now the might-have-been: the

little touches of English chintz and pottery that she must have added to her hotel bedroom to make it like home; the warm nest of spinsterly living into which she would eventually wind herself. So often this is the way with solitary Englishwomen of character who retire abroad: they harden like the autumnal beads at their throat into hard little wax pellets that no heat will ever melt again, they turn into a self-supporting wholesome substance that can never take anything in, nor be taken in, again.

At this moment then, when there was still a foot space in the door, my uncle Otway must have stepped into Cynthia's life.

'When I first saw him dear,' she told me, 'I thought he was the most wonderful creature I had ever set eyes on; from that moment I knew that nothing could ever be the same for me again.' She bloomed backwards now, and it was as if this second flowering that had come to her so long ago in Ibiza had now reached its second summer with the first shrivellings of autumn touching it.

It was late afternoon, and the delicate, work-reddened hands poised like scarlet butterflies over the tea-table. The moss roses painted on the Swansea wall plates came suddenly alive in her usually pale cheeks, the morning star that she grew in pots on the window sill was reflected for an instant in her stone-coloured eyes. 'I loved him without reservation; I was quite certain of myself from the first moment I set eyes on him. Oh! there had been others, in fact there was someone else about at the time of whom I was quite fond, but that's another story. Otway didn't ask me to marry him for several years, but it didn't seem to matter; I was content just to be near him and to catch the crumbs.'

I thought, looking at her then, after she had finished speaking, that it had not been art or craft that she had used in her gradual envelopment of my uncle, but indestructible patience that went beyond the boundaries of pride and hope.

Jasper, when he had begun to notice the absence of invitations to my uncle's flat, began to develop with me a technique of communication that was founded on disapproval. The material for this interplay was the intricacies and variabilities of the relationship between Uncle Otway and Cynthia. He would strike up an attitude of shocked amazement when I reported that the flat was full of young women in whom I was sure my uncle took more than just a casual interest. Egged on by his applause, I began out of the substance of my resentment to fabricate scenes of my middle-aged uncle surrounded by these prancing fillies; and each time Jasper would roar with laughter, giving a feeling of completion that somehow, at other times, our relationship seemed to lack.

'The fellow's a joke,' he would say, dispelling the age gap between us, strengthening any doubts as to the seriousness of his intentions towards me. 'But by Jove, he ought to be horse-whipped for fooling around treating Cynthia like that.'

I was on these occasions exultant, drunk with hope, for there is no feeling more heady than the wholehearted disapproval of one's neighbour. In this case too, a further miracle was effected: the impossible bridging of the years that bind and separate one generation of a family from another.

Normally it is not possible to treat someone of one's parents' age as an equal; but with Jasper it was different. With our jokes and underhand criticism of his contemporary, my uncle, we became like little children huddled together at the top of the nursery stairs eavesdropping and sniggering at the grown-ups.

That was our first summer together: the first taste for me of primrose warmth deepening to the heavy sweetness of honey. The flowering trees at Kew and Hampton Court were like top-heavy and wilting brides whose lacy whiteness clung, then slipped from their green shoulders and scattered over the fine yellow gravel of the paths, so neatly reminiscent of graveyard and hospital walk.

Jasper had too, what I found to be an added fascination: a sharp eye for the quaintly detailed, even though it be slightly macabre. He went to enormous pains to point out to me, in the London Museum, the rusty smudges that still showed on the blue woven singlet worn by Charles I at his execution: 'That's the place where the blood actually spurted when the axe fell.' He had passed his thin pointed tongue along his lips, and we had moved to the next display case. Then picking out the little humped boots, 'They say the fellow only had feet the size of an infant's,' he had explained. 'They had to weight him down with lead like a spinning top to keep him upright.'

The weight of the slowly moving ship easing its way out of the harbour of Barcelona stirs beneath us. Stephen is quick to mark out a place for us with the luggage on the raised surface of the battened-down hatch; here at least we will be able to stretch out without being walked over. A group of blond men and women establish themselves in the far corner; with blankets and lilos, a small spirit stove, they show up the flaws in our improvised travel equipment. We discover that they are German.

The vanishing city grows golden in the sunset, all the white roofs and walls touched with fire, unbelievably mellow and tender in outline; the remembrance of the glare and gritty discomfort of the streets is washed away.

The wind is like a cloth of silk, it has no sharp edges; we give ourselves up to the broad iron band across the hatch and allow it to divide one end of our spines from the other. Later with the excitement ebbing, and the drop in temperature of the blood, I find that it is almost impossible to get off to sleep; I roll my feet in a woollen cardigan and cover my shoulders with an overcoat, but the cold has settled into me and the garments slip away time after time from my rigid unfeeling limbs. Stephen is breathing steadily at my side, his loosely tucked overcoat emanates a constant warmth; he does not even stir from the contact of my cold hand.

Occasionally sheeted over by a thin layer of sleep, I imagine that I can still look up into the white bubbly surface of the top deck that makes a roof over us; then straight out through the railings over the black sea. Only waking sharply when the coat slips off, do I realise it to have been the light of a dream, for the ship is wrapt in darkness, but for one weak bulb left burning in the saloon. With this imposed solitude – the last person left awake – it is but a step to being the last person left alive in the world. How easy to slip silently through the wide railings unheeded; in the morning, unaccounted for. Like Cynthia after her first night in the earth, the waking could be as unexpected.

In the weak light of the dawn there appears against the sky the shadow of a long mountain range; grey and precise as a film negative, they look as barren as volcanic eruptions. But as we draw nearer the coastline the colours develop. A stubble of olive trees clutch into the red earth; the sun glitters on remotely scattered buildings – square blocks of salt, set into the wooded hillsides. There is no grouping of houses that would suggest a town, or even a village.

'If you ever go to Ibiza,' Cynthia had said to me, never supposing that I would have either the money or the enterprise to do so – and very naturally cherishing the exclusiveness that could not be spoilt by realistic comparison; 'you will be surprised how the capital and port of the island is suddenly upon you. One moment you will be following a range of endless mountains, and the next after rounding a point where a lighthouse stands, you will be in the harbour and looking up to a town whose houses cling like seagulls to the sides of a pointed hill, and crowned by a fortress and citadel that circle the cathedral.'

I had discovered even at this advanced stage of her self-imposed austerity that there was a vein of soft white chalkiness not very far below the surface that acted as an alkali on her increasingly acid nature; that sometimes the most cynical observations could be diverted into the soft flapping of a dove's wings. It was easy to bring tears to her large eyes, but it must be for a sufficiently small reason, like a childish effort thwarted. Real disaster simply hardened her; in most cases she considered it was well deserved.

Now, as Stephen and I stand at the rails of the ship becoming accustomed, a little bored, by the unchanging coastline, I wonder if the headland and lighthouse do really exist, or whether they too may have been a pinnacle of retreat from the hard work and poverty of the West Kensington flat – whether the white houses clinging to the hill were only shallow pulses that beat in sudden creative ecstasy within the delicate hollows of her small skull.

We walk to the stern of the ship and look back at the foaming peacock's tail we leave behind, at what is passing rather than what is to come. Suddenly Stephen says: 'Let's go to the front again. I think the course has changed. Did you feel it?'

Jasper was on to me about my eye before we had known each other three months. His approach was tactful but adamant: 'You simply must have it done; apart from what it looks like, it's bad for you to feel that you're different from other girls.'

I thought, he is a perfectionist and it is his way of saying that he wishes his possessions to be flawless. I read into the gentle coaxing, subtleties that went far beyond the limited feelings that one human being can have for another. When he said, 'I want to pay for you to have it done comfortably, Hatty,' I accepted it as a bridal veil. So, one dark November evening I found myself in a room leading off one of the centrally heated tunnels of the Middlesex Hospital.

He came to see me the day after the operation. I lay in a white iron bedstead, one eye covered and the other weakly watering in sympathy, and I tried to feel the moisture of reciprocated love in the papery dryness of his lined hand.

There was a second spring before the first threat of winter coldness in the relationship.

Up until that moment, except within the secrecy of my own interior monologues, I had been unable to bring myself to ever openly call him by his Christian name: I would hesitate when about to address an envelope and then with a bravado that was tingling with self-conscious uncertainty write the name *Jasper* rather more heavily than the Lomax.

We lay one afternoon dozing on the top of his day-bed in the large furnished room he rented when he was in London, just off the Earls Court Road.

'I notice, Hatty,' he said softly into my ear, 'that you have never called me by my Christian name; and although I think I can guess the reason for this, don't you think Jassy would be a little less impersonal now and then?'

This, I remember, was a shock; it made me immediately self-conscious both for his sake as well as for my own. It made me raise myself on my elbow and pull at the rumpled skirt of my dress and drag it further down over my bare knees. All at once it became imperative that I should stand up and be at an advantage. Before I rolled off the bed I noticed with cold detachment the corrugation of lines that ran like puckered stitching across his forehead, the pronounced widow's peak that I could now see was accentuated with the razor. I began to hate him for his turkey's neck and protruding Adam's apple.

But he was ahead of me, sensitive as a professional diviner; he was on his feet too, stretching his arms above his head; he filled in the square of window space with the width of his great muscled shoulders. Then going to the chest-of-drawers, he pulled out a bright blue spotted scarf and looped it casually, but with perfect precision, round his neck in sailor fashion. I was swept back into the deep water; now well beyond the depth when it would be possible to put foot to ground. 'Darling,' I said muzzily, 'I'll call you anything you like, or perhaps just "darling" for ever.'

I gave too much, unknowingly, yet I was pleased with myself for the generosity and the sound of the term of affection so fresh on my lips. But the crafty teddy bear who had wound the spring up to go so far, and no further, became suddenly wary, perhaps shocked at the giving. 'Come on,' he said smiling down at me from the summit of his full age, holding a surprise for the child behind his back, 'let's go gay, a little music and some dinner in Soho, with a bottle of Rosé d'Anjou.'

It was after that, some time between the stunted summer and prolonged autumn that I began knowingly to deceive myself. I still visited my uncle and his wife, now more and more for the reason of bringing to life something I knew to be fading in front of my eyes. I spoke to Cynthia on all occasions when there was doubt in my mind; like a moth I went straight towards the flame that would destroy me, listening with rapt attention to the words and tiny shafts that fell from her lips. Sometimes she seemed to torment me, but she would not let me die.

'He would be a fool to miss the chance of marrying you,' she would say, bringing to birth the thin phantasy that could hardly survive on its own within me. Later I was to discover that this was only a cue for me to commit myself still further, adding to the already growing heap of indiscretions and follies.

'Do you think that perhaps he doesn't say anything because of the difference in our ages?' I had asked her once as I sat in her drawing-room, dazed by the warmth of her sympathy and the flickering jets of the gas fire. Now, it was in this very room that I actually lived through the motions of my romantic phases with Jasper relying on Cynthia to extend the possibilities of the future by sustaining the actualities of the past.

Cynthia had her own difficulties. My uncle, now finally retired from his Staff job, found himself the recipient of a shrunken income that was the disability pension of a retired lieutenant-colonel. Unbeknown to him, she now put her child in a State day nursery and went out in the mornings to work in the houses of other people, sweeping and dusting. Yet she was always in and installed by the fire with the boy by the time he came in from his club after tea. So she supplemented their income, and he not knowing of the little inflow of money, thought her a miracle-maker and loved her the more for it. All this I knew, and found it hard to accept. If it had been in conjunction with anyone else but my uncle I should have seen it in the true light of heroism; as it was she was overshadowed, blighted. She both infected and was affected by him; as his temples narrowed and he squared his jaw in disapproval of me, so I repulsed them both, and dug my feet more firmly into the awful certainty of the shifting sands.

The island is like everything of picture-book quality that I have always wished to believe in: the mysterious paths leading through planes of extraordinary happiness to security off the page, the most powerful safety-valve of escape to the childish eye. Now the richness of colour and texture are here beneath my hands and feet; yet it is not the fresh greenness of England that is so quickly drained away from one's vision, leaving a tattering of rags on the stick branches, nor the first pale flutter of yellow that follows so slowly yet so temporarily. Here everything is thicker, deeper and more sustained. The loud pedal full on and never the foot raised. There is no intermediary season, no bareness, no rags.

The village of Santa Eulalia, ten kilometres west of the port, takes us two hours to reach. Our hotel proprietor who is at the landing stage to meet us in a battered car, drives to the market place of the town; then 'Un momento,' he says, slipping from the seat and leaves us for more than sixty minutes in the deepening glare.

At first we look every five minutes at the clock on the dashboard; then lie back in resignation against the dusty sour-smelling upholstery, the impatience fading away into the sun. Who does time belong to, I begin to wonder, that we should barter over the minutes under this clear blue sky?

The entrance to the village is as sudden as the approach to the port has been. After driving along straight roads, poplar-lined leading to nowhere, there is an ancient low arched bridge; a shallow flowing river below has smoothed the brown homely rocks to a domestic comfort. Growing thickly at the water's edge and even over the width of the river on the larger stones whose hollows have been silted with a thin layer of mud, blooms the wild pinkness of the oleander: the flower that Cynthia carried in her mind all those hard years in the felted depths of Stamford Gardens.

Trailing banks of giant blue convolvulus, purple bougainvillea twisted into the formal intricacy of black wrought iron – all hang downwards towards the sea. Lemons in the hotel garden, still green, but ripening in patches, and below the shelving gardens, the wilder unfenced land parcelled into small plots, sloping away to the sea's edge: everywhere the stunted grey of the olive trees. With our small rationed vision we are like greedy children looking everywhere for more and more; we stare into the brilliance like seers, seeking an unsimple and deeper quality; when we do not find it, we call it surfeit.

In the heat of the siesta we lie panting for breath on the narrow beds, hardly longer than cots; the first meal in the hotel has been entirely yellow: fried eggs on a bank of saffron-coloured rice, and yellow plums whose unripe flesh still clung to the stone.

'Do you think we shall be able to come to grips with all this beauty and leisure?' I ask Stephen. 'I wish I could find a piano in the village.'

'Why don't you take the opportunity of soaking up the brandy at threepence a glass?' he answers me from where he floats beneath the first layers of a deepening sleep.

After a few days, I find myself watching for the post to come and bring letters from Hampstead and Bloomsbury. When there is nothing, there is a terrible finality about it, for there are only three posts a week.

One day Amy writes in her square-nibbed script: 'I ordered a white sheaf for Cynthia from you; carnations filled in with white lilac and gypsophila'.

After the first six months of our knowing each other, I found it impossible to carry within my mind a clear picture of myself in relation to Jasper. My vision was blurred, because I had outwardly accepted the state. I would have noticed nothing except drastic change, or sudden removal. Small things began to gain significance: the fact that he would run at my side without the audible breathing that I associated with age, made me eulogise extravagantly: 'You must have been a cross-country runner, really darling, you're like an Achilles.' And from thence developed the joke motion that we called secretly 'the Achilles hop' – a long-legged stride that took us on springy legs to bus stop and underground station, causing my heart to beat with a steady excitement.

With Cynthia though, there was clarity and discernment. Many times she would stress, unmercifully I thought, the thinness of his neck, the permanent droop of his shoulders, and the thick yellowing of his grey thatch that he took such pains to dress, peering (as I had often seen him do) into his three-sided looking-glass to get a good view of the back. All these things, superimposed by Cynthia over the real picture, I stored up, and chose privately to magnify for his belittlement;

as if by doing so I insured a personal detachment. In her way Cynthia helped me to stay the process of advancement, perhaps also she prolonged the pain.

I found too that I had an ally in Ted. 'You're becoming quite a popsy,' he told me, 'with those whirlpool eyes, and all that paint on your face.' It was now quite simple to go out with him, and lay aside the gnawing anxiety of whether one could think of anything to say that would not be overridden or dissected into minute particles of stupidity.

I had practically abandoned my piano at home; sometimes I strummed for the pleasure of my aunt and uncle. Jasper was almost completely tone deaf, but I did not judge him for it. Instead I kept my talent that he could not share, well in abeyance, bringing it out only occasionally when he was not there.

Ted heard me play the Beethoven Appassionata one day at Cynthia's, and said, 'You have passion and style Hatty, sometimes you play like a great artist, and sometimes like a half-wit with no co-ordination or understanding.'

I accepted his assessment because it was valid, even it seemed the words of praise. It was possible to accept the full truth of half artist or genius *manqué* now that it no longer mattered.

Jasper had a house on the edge of the Essex marshes. A rambling white-washed farmstead surrounded by chestnut palings, it stood in a jungle of cultivated disorderliness. Coarse salt-tipped grass grew at the edge of the paths and giant poppies that had seeded themselves into the suffocating undergrowth of St John's wort and bindweed. The garden sank into a hollow where there was shelter from the North Sea winds.

Here on a bed of wild roses and convolvulus suckers, we would lay our plumped-up lilos, and look out across the course of the flat brown river whose level sank so low in the summer drought. It reminded him of India, he said; and although I had been born there I wished he would not tell me that there was anywhere else on earth that could compare with this private paradise.

I wondered sometimes if perhaps he might have ever contracted a marriage with a Eurasian, and that this was the reason for his silence. My grandfathers on both sides had done this, though until the advent of Ted I had always been led to believe that their brides had been a Sicilian and a Spaniard of noble birth. 'Haven't you seen the bridal photographs in Otway's album, my dear? They're as black as your hat.'

I could not even bring myself to expose this fact to Jasper; it was too near the bone. He had given me my eye, and for this I would never be able to repay him.

He must have felt the weight and pressure of my unasked questions; because of them I found very little else to say.

One day in the garden, he suggested that it would be a good thing if I joined a club for young people. 'Cynthia's son should be able to help you over that,' he said, 'although I've always suspected the fellow of being a little red, and we don't want you mixed up with Bolshies, do we Hatty?' I saw fit in a moment of temper to bring out some of the catch-phrases of Ted's that had lodged at the back of my mind without use until just such an occasion; the clarity of his suggestion caused me to lash about me with these blunted weapons of whose strength I had no idea.

Now there was misunderstanding at all levels.

On the train to London we hardly spoke a word; dry-eyed and cold with apprehension, we parted on Liverpool Street station, no word, no renewal of faith, nothing.

So it was winter again, and the time passing with an existence eked out on so few meetings that they could no longer be called consecutive. I knew that even in conversation I could not say: 'I see Jasper now and then,' but rather: 'I don't see Jasper very often now.'

One afternoon I remember particularly. It had been an iron-hard January, the gas pressure so low that I walked about the house in rubbed fur boots to keep my feet warm. I still continued the painful operation of telephoning to keep the contact alive, even at widely spaced intervals; in this I was influenced unconsciously by Cynthia and her long patience with my uncle before they married. 'If you want something enough there is nothing that can stop you getting it except yourself,' she had once said.

I went to the telephone and spoke to Jasper. 'You must come to dinner tonight,' I said, 'I've got something very special, a bottle of Imperial Tokay, and this is just the day to drink it,' I added with the kind of reckless humour that is borne on the wings of hysteria.

Afterwards, as I went about the task of preparing the meal, I felt all the apprehension and strain it had cost me to make the call after a three weeks' silence.

When he arrived, he was blue with cold – it seemed I could do nothing to produce warmth. He kept his muffler on all through dinner, and I watched the food grow thick as white jade on our plates between each mouthful. Even the precious wine had no fire in it, and remained dead and frosted in the glasses.

I think he felt for me then, in my ugly and exposed dilemma; as he sat on the sofa, rubbing his hands in a perpetual washing movement, his stiff winged collar made me think of an elderly solicitor, a commissioner for oaths, a close friend of the family.

'My dear,' he had said as he was going, 'fond as I am of you, I can't have you spending all your hard-earned pennies on me.'

'You see how it was?' I say to Stephen one morning after breakfast when we are sitting out above the beach on the spongy bank of sea-dross, brindled as a hedgehog's back, that fringes the whole island between the fields and the sea. 'I had to go on telling Cynthia everything; there was simply no one else. Mother had gone to live with Great-aunt in Salisbury, and anyway there wasn't much understanding between us since I'd had my eye done. You know, she never once said she was pleased or that she noticed the difference.'

'She was probably irritated that she hadn't been able to pay for it herself, that's nearer the truth,' Stephen answers, dispelling the cobwebs of resentment that could spin themselves across the lightness of the sky. Now as he lies beside me in the full blaze of the sun it seems to me that for the first time in his life he too is worming his way out of the chrysalis; his blue trunks expose a scar below the navel that is still a livid red, unlike the golden brown on the rest of his body. He once told me that it was the beginning of a rupture he got in the army from unloading a heavy truck; but I feel that it is a late snapping of the umbilical cord.

I pull my big-brimmed hat further over my face; I cannot really afford to let the lines at the corners of my eyes become too pronounced. It is strange to think of the mild effort I make now to preserve the smoothness of my skin, that before I had regarded as only a blankness of countenance: the balance is completely reversed; and with this new contentment I can afford the generosity of recollection. If I went to see Jasper today, he might be quite pleased to see me, I think. Poor Jasper in his Sydenham boarding-house, riddled with arthritis. Why did he never marry anyone, I wonder? Perhaps he really hated women in a permanent relationship except as sisters or mothers.

Stephen is now deeply asleep; the thickness of his heavy lids screen him from the glare that exposes to me every plane and crevice of his dark face. How strange has been the reassembling and solution of our lives; Cynthia newly dead, myself newly married, Jasper a resigned invalid. The pain and the urgency had gone for ever. Did nobody love anyone in those days, or only themselves? Was it all an illusion of youth?

We find the time-lapse between breakfast and lunch at three o'clock a great discipline. We go from extremes of hunger to complete indifference about food, and, as this takes place, so our stomachs shrink, so that when the time comes we pick like birds at the food before us.

Today there is a whole pile of letters and papers for us. We fall upon them like wild animals and take them into the dining-room with us.

There is a letter for me from Ted. We have always remained friendly and he never took sides in the trouble between his mother and myself. Once, in the war, he made me an offer. 'Not exactly marriage, because as you know I don't hold with such medieval conceptions, but we would make a unit, set up in rooms somewhere – a revolutionary monogamy. You could pay half the rent,' he had said.

Today his letter, three closely written pages, is full of description and ironic humour; a transparent covering over the gap caused by his mother's death:

> 'All the family, including your mother, turned up in black crêpe and veils. You should have seen them pushing for the best place in the churchyard. There was quite a little incident at one moment when the undertakers had to drive them back from the crumbling raw earth.
>
> 'Step-Pa, very upright and soldierly. The tears he shed were small and steely. I felt like a midget beside him – also I was the only member of the party in tweeds.
>
> 'I noticed Jasper during the proceedings standing very much apart from the rest of us, very tottery on two sticks. And now Hatty, here is *an occurrence* for you, something spooky to give you the creeps under all that Mediterranean blue.